"Why did you bring us to your home?"

"No one will ever think to look here. You'll be safe," Dillon said, his gaze confident.

Safe.

Jacqueline glanced down at Amanda once again, at her little girl's tired eyes, glassy and wide with fear. She wanted so much to believe they were safe with Dillon.

But could she, with a murderer out there she knew nothing about and a man protecting them who was on his own personal crusade?

She once again allowed her gaze to meet his. Two things were clear. There was more to this case than Dillon was telling her. And there was more driving him than dedication to his job.

She had a lot of questions for the cowboy district attorney. And if she was going to keep her baby safe, she needed answers....

Dear Harlequin Intrigue Reader,

Yet again we have a power-packed lineup of fantastic books for you this month, starting with the second story in the new Harlequin continuity series TRUEBLOOD, TEXAS. *Secret Bodyguard* by B.J. Daniels brings together an undercover cop and a mobster's daughter in a wary alliance in order to find her baby. But will they find a family together before all is said and done?

Ann Voss Peterson contributes another outstanding legal thriller to Harlequin Intrigue with *His Witness, Her Child*. Trust me, there's nothing sexier than a cowboy D.A. who's as tough as nails on criminals, yet is as tender as lamb's wool with women and children. Except...

One of Julie Miller's Taylor men! This month read about brother Brett Taylor in *Sudden Engagement*. Mystery, matchmaking—it's all part and parcel for any member of THE TAYLOR CLAN.

Finally, I'm thrilled to introduce you to Mallory Kane, who debuts at Harlequin Intrigue with *The Lawman Who Loved Her*. Hang on to your hat—and your heart. This story—and this hunky hero—will blow you away.

Round up all four! And be on the lookout next month for a *new* Harlequin Intrigue trilogy by Amanda Stevens called EDEN'S CHILDREN.

Happy reading,

Denise O'Sullivan
Associate Senior Editor
Harlequin Intrigue

HIS WITNESS, HER CHILD

ANN VOSS PETERSON

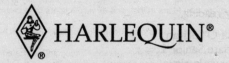

TORONTO • NEW YORK • LONDON
AMSTERDAM • PARIS • SYDNEY • HAMBURG
STOCKHOLM • ATHENS • TOKYO • MILAN • MADRID
PRAGUE • WARSAW • BUDAPEST • AUCKLAND

ISBN 0-373-22618-7

HIS WITNESS, HER CHILD

ABOUT THE AUTHOR

Ever since she was a little girl making her own books out of construction paper, Ann Voss Peterson wanted to write. So when it came time to choose a major at the University of Wisconsin, creative writing was her only choice. Of course, writing wasn't a *practical* choice—one needs to earn a living. So Ann found jobs ranging from proofreading legal transcripts to working with quarter horses to washing windows. But no matter how she earned her paycheck, she continued to write the type of stories that captured her heart and imagination—romantic suspense. Ann lives near Madison, Wisconsin, with her husband, her toddler son, her Border collie and her quarter horse mare.

Books by Ann Voss Peterson

HARLEQUIN INTRIGUE
579—INADMISSIBLE PASSION
618—HIS WITNESS, HER CHILD

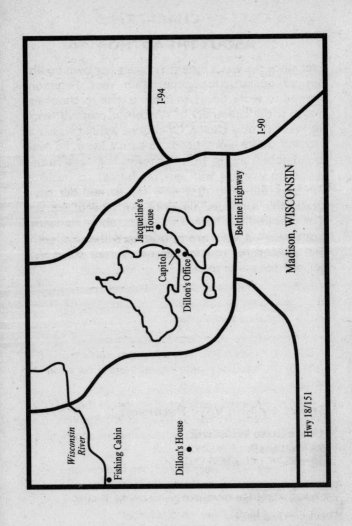

Madison, WISCONSIN

I-94

I-90

Beltline Highway

Jacqueline's House

Capitol

Dillon's Office

Hwy 18/151

Wisconsin River

Fishing Cabin

Dillon's House

CAST OF CHARACTERS

Dillon Reese—An assistant D.A. who didn't only want justice, he needed it. So when he lost his star witness in his latest murder trial, he vowed to catch the killer at whatever cost.

Jacqueline Schettler—She was a mother first and foremost and she had to protect her child, even if that meant going against Assistant D.A. Dillon Reese, the compelling crusader for justice who desperately needed her young daughter's testimony.

Amanda Schettler—An innocent child—and witness to a brutal murder. The only sanctuary she had now was in her mother's arms.

Buck Swain—A war hero turned murderer who had either an uncanny knack for staying one step ahead of the D.A.'s office—or an informer on the inside.

Neil Fitzroy—The Dane County District Attorney had a bright political future ahead of him. But just how far would he go to protect it?

Dex Harrington—As Fitzroy's greatest rival for the D.A.'s job, Dex might have a stake in keeping Buck Swain a free man—and Fitzroy's office mired in scandal.

Kit Ashner—It wasn't easy for a woman in the D.A.'s office—not even a woman as tough as Kit. But was she the type to leak secrets to keep herself ahead of her colleagues?

Dale Kearney—The fiery-haired cop had crossed paths with the murderer during his days in the military. Would his soldier's bond with Swain cause him to betray his buddies on the force?

Al Mylinski—The only man Dillon Reese trusted with his life. But was that trust misplaced?

To Cole, who made the writing of this book
both a challenge and a joy.

Chapter One

Jacqueline Schettler pushed the gas pedal to the floor and steered frantically through the icy streets of Madison, Wisconsin. Heat blasted from the car's dashboard vents, drying her tears. Tonight her worst fears had become reality. The whispered warnings on the telephone, the cut-and-paste notes stuck to the front door—a half-dozen threats had come to fruition. Mark, her ex-husband, was dead. Murdered on the eve of his testimony in the Swain murder trial.

A block away from the Schettler Brew Pub, Jacqueline stomped on the brake and swung her car to the curb. She threw open the door and climbed into the frigid night. "I'm coming, baby. Just hang on. Mommy will be there very soon. Mommy will make you safe."

The moment she'd received her little girl's frantic phone call, she knew Amanda was in danger. Although only seven years old, her daughter wasn't given to flights of imagination. She wouldn't make up a story like the one she'd told between sobs tonight. Something had happened at the pub, all right. Mark was dead. And unless Jacqueline reached the pub before the police questioned Amanda, her little girl was bound to be next.

Heart pounding, she ran the remaining distance, the cold air making her throat and lungs ache. Nearing the beer garden behind the pub, she slowed to a brisk walk. Police cars huddled around the gated entrance, their red and blue lights pulsing off the pub's yellow brick like the swirling lights of a carnival.

Dread pierced her heart. Had the police found Amanda?

Please God, don't let me be too late.

Jacqueline raised her parka's hood over her head with trembling fingers. Bowing her head to hide her face, she shoved her hands into her pockets. She couldn't let anyone see her. Or, God forbid, recognize her. If they did, they would ask questions. They would put the pieces together.

They would find Amanda. They would learn what she'd seen. As with Mark, the district attorney would insist she testify. And once that happened, no one could keep her safe. Not the district attorney's office, not the police, maybe not even God himself.

The cobblestone beer garden seethed with police and evidence technicians snapping pictures and taking measurements. The low hum of their words floated on the biting wind. Their voices were thin, hushed, a tone reserved for the aftermath of tragedy.

Jacqueline dodged behind a row of Dumpsters and scurried up a short flight of stairs to a little-used side door. She pulled her old key chain from her pocket. Finding the right key, she opened the door, slipped inside and closed the door quietly behind her.

Like ozone after a thunderstorm, the heavy odor

of deep-fried food hung in the still air of the kitchen. Nothing but silence came from the cooks' line or the prep area. A cold shiver crept up her spine. She hadn't set foot inside her father's old pub since she'd signed over control to Mark as part of the divorce settlement nearly six months ago. And despite the threats, she'd never imagined she'd return under such circumstances. She stepped carefully across the expanse of greasy red tile and toward what used to be her father's office.

A feeble blue light glowed from the crack under the office door. She unlocked the door and turned the knob, the brass slick under her fingers. After one last glance around the deserted kitchen, she ducked inside the office and closed the door safely behind her.

"Amanda? Are you here, sweetheart?" Jacqueline held her breath. *Amanda has to be here. Please. The police can't have found her.*

A rustling sound rose from under the desk. "Mommy?" Faint and tremulous, Amanda's voice was little more than a mew.

Still, it was the sweetest sound Jacqueline had ever heard. She shoved the desk chair out of the way. Falling to her knees, she gathered her little girl into her arms.

Amanda clung to her like a frightened kitten. She gasped air in hiccuping sobs. Her heart pattered frantically in her little chest.

Jacqueline squeezed her tight until her seven-year-old's heartbeat melded with her own. She breathed deeply, drawing in Amanda's fresh, little-girl scent. "I'm here, sweetheart. I'm here."

Night air and the hum of voices drifted through

the open window, snapping Jacqueline back to the situation at hand. Soon the police would extend their evidence gathering to the rest of the brew pub. They would search Mark's office. She had to get her daughter out of the building before the police spotted them. Before they learned Amanda had witnessed her daddy's murder.

Before the murderer set his mind to silencing Amanda the way he'd silenced Mark.

Jacqueline kissed Amanda's cheek, tasting the salty tears—her daughter's and her own. "We're going home now, punkin. And we have to be very quiet."

Amanda raised her blue eyes, tears clinging to her long lashes. After a few hiccuping breaths, she found her voice. "I stayed in the office in the dark like you told me on the phone. I locked the door."

"You're a good girl. You did everything right."

Amanda nodded, but didn't relax her clinging grip. She buried her face in Jacqueline's neck.

The voices in the beer garden seemed to grow louder. Closer.

Jacqueline stood and hoisted her daughter to her hip. They couldn't stay here a minute longer. She needed to get Amanda out unseen while she still had the chance.

She moved to the open window to see what was happening outside. The worst thing she could do was run blindly out of the building and smack into a throng of cops. Smoothing her hand over Amanda's silky hair, she held her little girl's head in place against her neck. Amanda didn't need to see the scene below the window. She'd already seen more horrors than anyone should see in a lifetime.

The beer garden glowed with the pale yellow light from old-fashioned lantern poles. Skeletons of dog-wood and cherry jutted from raised flower beds, now barren and dusted with snow. In the middle of the activity, in the middle of the courtyard, Mark's still figure lay on the cold cobblestone.

Her heart constricted.

He lay on his back, his green eyes open in a blank stare, his face flashing pale with every burst of a camera's flashbulb. A thick ribbon of red slashed his neck. Blood stained his blond ponytail.

She closed her eyes, but it was no use. The sight had burned into her memory forever, an incarnation of the horrible nightmares she'd endured since Mark had witnessed Buck Swain disposing of those blood-soaked clothes over a year ago.

Jacqueline clenched her teeth and opened her eyes, staring at Mark's body. If only he'd listened to her when the phone calls started coming, when she'd found the threatening notes taped to the front door. But he'd been so caught up in the bright lights and celebrity that accompanied a war hero's murder trial that the well-being of his family had finished a distant second. Thanks to the urging of the assistant district attorney prosecuting the case, Mark had been more than willing to place interviews on the local TV news and a bustling pub business above his daughter's safety. And his own.

The past few months when the threats had slowed to a trickle and then stopped altogether, she'd let herself believe the danger was over. She'd even allowed

Amanda to spend this evening with her father when
an accident at work had forced Jacqueline to stay
late. Between the cessation of the threats and Mark's
continued police protection, she'd believed her
daughter would be safe. She couldn't have been more
wrong.

A low moan issued from her throat. Even though
she'd never forgive Mark for risking Amanda's life,
even though their marriage had been over long before
the divorce, she'd never wish this on him. Death.
Murder. She ached to run to him, to cradle his head
in her arms, to cry for him. But it was too late. She
couldn't help him now.

But she could save their daughter.

Jacqueline forced herself to concentrate on the var-
ious locations of the officers and technicians below.
They hadn't spread out from the beer garden to the
walkway behind the Dumpsters. If she left now, she
could exit the way she came.

Holding Amanda close, she spun away from the
window and strode to the door. Cracking it open, she
peered into the kitchen. No sound, no movement.
Drawing in a deep breath, she crept into the kitchen
and closed the office door behind her.

A cold draft chilled her to the bone. The side door
stood wide open. She gasped. She'd closed it when
she'd sneaked in. She was sure of it. That left only
one alternative. Someone had entered the kitchen behind her.

Surely it couldn't be the murderer. He would be
long gone by now. The police? She couldn't breathe.
She couldn't think. She held Amanda tightly in her

arms. She had to get out of the pub. And she had to do it now.

She bolted through the open door and raced down the cement steps. She crouched behind the Dumpsters.

The odor of spent hops wafted from the steel bins, clogging in the back of her throat. The red and blue lights of idling police cars flashed in her eyes. Exhaust fumes hung in the frosty air.

Amanda whimpered into the hollow of Jacqueline's neck, a small sound like the coo of a pigeon.

Jacqueline smoothed her trembling fingers over her daughter's hair, trying to quiet her. Several police officers stood at the beer garden's gate. Close enough to hear any sound. Close enough to see her make a break for the street.

Jacqueline bit the inside of her bottom lip until the coppery tang of blood tinged her mouth. She had to get past the gate without anyone seeing them. But how?

A large black pickup roared into the mouth of the beer garden and screeched to a halt. A lone figure dismounted from the vehicle. Tall and imposing in a black oilskin duster, Assistant District Attorney Dillon Reese surveyed the crime scene through squinted black eyes.

Jacqueline slunk lower behind the Dumpsters. Dillon Reese. A shiver started at the nape of her neck and worked its way down her spine. Sweat broke out on the palms of her hands. He'd always affected her that way, from the first time she'd met him. He was larger than life. He didn't seem to belong to marble halls and paneled courtrooms. He looked more like a lawman straight out of the Old West than a prosecuting attorney working in the shadow of Wisconsin's capitol.

And his voice. He had used his rich baritone and slow Texas drawl to convince Mark to testify, to promise her that Mark would be safe. And at first she'd believed him. Every word.

More than that. She'd admired him. His dedication, his drive, his need to do the right thing. Her marriage to Mark clearly heading for divorce, she'd even allowed herself to fantasize about what her life would be like with a man like Dillon.

Then the threats had started. Threats to Mark's life, threats to Amanda. And Dillon had continued to encourage Mark to testify, continued to push him, laying one promise on top of another.

And now Mark was dead.

She gritted her teeth. Mark was dead because Dillon had to do the right thing. He had to have justice. And now Amanda was in danger, as well. Dillon's promises had turned out to be nothing but lies. And he was a liar, pure and simple. A liar with a voice as deep and smoky as a mesquite fire.

Duster flapping behind him, he strode into the beer garden, the heels of his snakeskin boots sounding on the cobblestones. All heads turned in his direction.

Now was her chance. Little did he know it, but he had provided her with the perfect diversion. Clutching Amanda tightly to her hip, she bolted across the street and raced down the block to the safety of her car. Above the tattoo of her heels on the sidewalk, above the ragged roar of her breathing, Dillon's empty promises echoed in her memory. "Your husband will be safe, ma'am. I can protect your family, ma'am.''

"Damn you, Dillon Reese," she whispered through clenched teeth. "Damn you to hell."

Chapter Two

Little Amanda Schettler looked up at Dillon, her eyes big and blue as a Texas sky, a well-loved stuffed horse wrapped in both arms. She was barely seven years old, her face baby plump, her features round like a pup's. The feeble morning sunlight filtering through a living-room window sparked a halo of sorrel highlights in her hair. "I saw the man kill my daddy."

Her thin little voice hit him with more force than a mule kick to the head. Anger blasted through him. Gut-wrenching anger with a chaser of guilt. Because of him, because he'd let down his guard, the little girl would go through the rest of her life haunted by the flick of a murderer's knife.

He stepped toward the little girl, the old Victorian's hardwood floor creaking under his boots. He hadn't gotten a wink of sleep all night thinking about the faint rap of running feet when he'd arrived at the Schettler Brew Pub and about the car streaking past moments later—a car that had looked suspiciously like Jacqueline Schettler's. He had come to the Schettler home this morning to confirm his ugly suspicion that little Amanda had been at the pub last night. And she had watched a man slit her daddy's throat.

He clenched his teeth until his jaw ached. Buck Swain would pay. Dillon would guaran-damn-tee it.

Biting back his anger, he crouched and studied Amanda from her own level. "Can you tell me what the man looked like, darlin'?"

Amanda blinked, her long golden lashes brushing pink cheeks. Lifting her chin, she stared past him and up at her mother.

Without turning around, he could picture the fear shining in Jacqueline Schettler's blue eyes, the color draining from her already pale skin. But her fear wouldn't last long. If he knew Jacqueline, she wouldn't let it. Her eyes were probably already narrowing into slits, her anger plunging into his back like a sharp blade.

He'd seen her turn fear into anger before. Like the night she'd received the first threatening phone call. When he'd rushed to her house, he'd found her alone and scared, hands shaking so badly she couldn't hold a glass of water. He'd held her in his arms until her trembling stopped, reluctant even then to let her go. Even after police officers had been posted outside her house, he'd stayed with her, sipping coffee and talking until dawn, when Mark had finally stumbled home.

That night there had been something between them, a connection, an intimacy he couldn't explain. Something held in check only by the wedding ring still on her finger.

But the threats had kept coming, and Jacqueline

had withdrawn. She'd grown distant toward him, cool. Then Swain had threatened her daughter. And after that she'd refused to see him or talk to him. Without her cooperation he had been unable to get Swain's bail revoked. With the threat to Amanda, his hat had changed from white to black.

And now he'd never be able to change it back.

Jacqueline was afraid for her daughter then, and she was doubly afraid for her daughter now. And he knew damn well that behind his back she was silently signaling the little girl to keep quiet.

Amanda swung her attention to Dillon, her fingers twisting a shank of hair into a tight little rope. Her gaze dropped to the colorful, hand-braided rug beneath her shoes. "I...I don't remember."

"See? She doesn't remember." Jacqueline stepped around him, close enough for him to catch her soft vanilla scent. She collected her daughter into the circle of her arms. Eyes narrowed to those damn little slits, she glared at him as if she wished him dead. "You've done your job. Now you can leave with a clear conscience."

He straightened and faced her. Clear conscience? Like hell. His conscience would never be clear. Not until his dying day. "I'm not going to just walk out the door, Jacqueline. You know that."

Her eyebrows pinched together. She glared at him, her expression as damning as a hangman's noose around his neck. "You promised to protect Mark. You promised he'd be safe."

He had promised. And he'd failed. He swallowed hard and looked her straight in the eye. "I'm sorry."

"It's too late to be sorry." She shook her head,

her chestnut hair rustling with the movement. "You shouldn't have let him give all those interviews. You shouldn't have let him put publicity for the brew pub ahead of his family's safety. You knew he was a loose cannon."

He held up his hands in a gesture of surrender. "If I could have hog-tied him, I would have. You have every right to be angry. Hell, you have every right to take it out of my hide."

The look in her eyes suggested she'd be willing to do just that. "Why was Mark at the pub last night? He was supposed to be at his condo watching Disney movies with Amanda. He was supposed to have a cop protecting him."

"Truth is, Jacqueline, I don't know. Maybe his protection was yanked because it had been so long since the last threat. Maybe the police got sloppy. Maybe I got sloppy. I should have made sure he was protected. I should have made sure he stayed put. It's my fault. I'm sorry."

She closed her eyes as if shutting out his words. "I don't want your apology. All I want is for you to leave us alone."

As much as he wanted to do what she asked, he couldn't leave them alone. Amanda was an eyewitness to murder. His best bet in a case with damn few leads. As of yet, the police had found no murder weapon, no fingerprints of value, nothing to point in the direction of the killer. Dillon knew who'd done it—Buck Swain's foul stench was all over this case—but knowing didn't do him a sliver of good. He couldn't prove it. Just as he couldn't prove Swain was the one who'd threatened Mark. Without the little girl's help, his case was so thin it couldn't cast a shadow. "I can't let a killer go free."

"You always do the right thing, don't you? No matter who might get hurt." She bit off her words, a note of irony in her voice. Slowly she opened her eyes. "The only thing you seem to really care about is justice."

Of course he cared about justice. He wouldn't be in this job if he didn't. But it was more than that. Much more. He'd admitted that to himself long ago. He didn't just care about justice—he needed it.

For Janey.

Of all people, he thought Jacqueline Schettler would understand his need. He thought she would want the same thing. Of course, since the divorce and for quite some time before, Mark Schettler hadn't been much of a family to Jacqueline. But he would always be family to her daughter. "Don't you want the man who killed your little girl's daddy to pay?"

She narrowed her eyes, but even her thick fringe of lashes couldn't hide the glint of indignation. "Of course I do."

"Then why aren't we communicating here?"

She reached down and brushed a strand of hair from her little girl's round cheek. The movement of her long, slender fingers was so soft and tender, he couldn't prevent the tightening at the back of his throat. When Jacqueline looked back at him, her finely chiseled features seemed to harden. Her eyes flashed with anger, hot as blue flame. "Making that man pay isn't the only issue. It isn't even the most important one."

He looked down at Amanda. Those innocent eyes.

Those round, sweet cheeks. His throat kinked into a knot, and tenderness swelled inside him. Of course to a mother, her little girl would be the *only* important issue. Especially a good mother like Jacqueline. "You don't have to worry. I'll make sure Amanda is safe. Your daughter here, she holds the key. One point of her finger, and we can get the guy who did this."

Amanda looked up at him, eyes huge and haunted, mouth drawn into a grim line. She clutched the stuffed horse in one hand, her other little hand balled into a fist by her side, her index finger stretching out into a point.

The sight hit him hard. That little finger with its pink nail polish. Her tight little knuckles as pale as paste. He clenched his jaw against the onslaught, but he couldn't take his eyes off her finger.

"Sweetheart." Jacqueline's husky contralto cracked with emotion. She knelt by Amanda's side. Squeezing her daughter, she whispered in the little girl's ear.

Amanda clutched her stuffed horse in both arms and reluctantly nodded. She tore herself from Jacqueline and dragged her feet down the hall, glancing over her shoulder every three steps as if to reassure herself that her mama hadn't deserted her as her daddy had.

Jacqueline watched every step her daughter took with such concern, Dillon could swear the little girl was walking a tightrope with no net underneath.

Maybe she was. And to Jacqueline Schettler it probably seemed as if he wanted to raise the tightrope to the highest point in the big top. Damn. If he could catch and prosecute the man who had killed Mark Schettler, without involving Amanda, he would do it as surely as he breathed. But right now the police had no other witnesses and no promising leads. If he wanted to rid the street of Buck Swain, he had to rely on Amanda.

As soon as the bedroom door thunked closed behind her daughter, Jacqueline faced him squarely. She was thinner than the last time he'd seen her, almost frail looking in a shapeless sweater and jeans. But Jacqueline Schettler wasn't frail. Far from it. Deep down, she was tough. Tough and plumb sexy. From her thick chestnut mane and expressive blue eyes to the passion that bubbled not far beneath her surface, she was some kind of woman. Her husky voice and light vanilla fragrance could charm a charging bull. She'd charmed him the first time he laid eyes on her.

Muscles tightened along her square jaw. Her hands balled into fists by her sides. "Putting Mark's murderer in prison is not as simple as pointing a finger, and you know it. Mark was murdered for pointing a finger. The same thing will *not* happen to Amanda."

"I can put the two of you in protective custody. I'll move you into a secured apartment and make sure you have 'round-the-clock police protection.''

"Why would any of that make a difference? Threats or no threats, Mark was supposed to have a cop by his side every time he set foot outside his condo until the trial was over. Last night he left his condo, and guess what? No cop. After what happened to Mark, why on earth would I agree to let you make my daughter a sitting duck?''

She drew in a breath of air and expelled it through tight lips. "You may not have noticed this, Dillon, but you're no Clint Eastwood and this is no spaghetti Western. In real life the cowboy with the swagger and the just cause doesn't always win in the end. You didn't win the last round, and I'd be a fool to bet my daughter's life that you'll win the next."

He stood tall and took her anger full in the gut. He'd earned it, after all. She deserved her chance to vent. But that didn't mean he was about to back down. "Damn straight I didn't win the last round. That's why nothing's going to keep me from winning the next. I aim to use every shred of power in the district attorney's office to personally make sure Amanda's safe."

Jacqueline crooked a delicate eyebrow. "Oh? Things are going to be different this time because you feel guilty? I don't think the world works that way. Besides, I don't buy your guilt act. I don't think you're interested in Amanda's well-being at all. I think you just want to salvage your case."

Hell yes, he wanted to salvage his case. *And* he wanted to keep Amanda safe. But not just because of guilt. He was no unfeeling robot. He cared what happened to his witnesses. How could he not care?

And if he was being honest with himself, this little girl was more than just a witness to him. This little girl and her mother were special. "Believe anything you damn well want. Either way, I give you my word. Amanda will be safe. There's a killer out there, Jacqueline. A killer who just might know your little girl was in the pub last night."

Her face grew pale, her eyes dark and wide. She

glanced toward the bedroom where her daughter had disappeared. "He couldn't know. If he did, don't you think he would have killed her last night? No. If Amanda doesn't show up on your witness list, he'll never know she saw him."

"You may be right. He may not know she saw him. But why take the chance? Come down to my office. Amanda can look through a photo lineup and give a videotaped deposition describing what she saw. Once her memories are on record, the murderer won't be able to gain anything by killing her. She'll be safe."

That damned square jaw of hers hardened like a drill sergeant's. "I doubt it's that easy. If it is, why didn't you have Mark give a deposition after he started getting the threats?"

"Mark didn't want Swain's lawyer cross-examining him. And once the death threats started, he feared that if Swain's attorney had access to him, Swain would, too. Without the cross, the deposition likely wouldn't have been admissible in court."

"Wouldn't that be a problem with Amanda's testimony, too?"

"The court is often more lenient with child witnesses."

She shook her head. "*Often* more lenient? But you don't really *know* if her videotaped testimony would be admissible or not, do you? Sorry, Dillon, that's not good enough. Amanda's not talking to anyone. If she's not a witness, she's not a threat."

"You're fooling yourself, Jacqueline. She's in danger whether she testifies or not. So why don't you let me make sure she's safe? Why don't you help me put Swain in prison where he can't hurt her or anyone else?''

''Don't you think I want to help? Don't you think I want the man who did this behind bars? Don't you think I want your promises to be real?'' She looked down at the woven rug beneath her feet. If he wasn't mistaken, a slight glistening of tears moistened the corners of her eyes and shimmered in her lower lashes. ''Please, Dillon. Please leave us alone.''

He gritted his teeth. He could handle her anger. He could handle her bitter words. He deserved them. But the sight of her tears, the sound of her whispered plea slashed into him, leaving a gaping wound. He reached out a hand, wanting to touch her, wanting to pull her into his arms, wanting to promise her everything would be okay.

But she'd never again trust a promise he made—she'd made that clear. And she sure as hell wouldn't accept his touch or his embrace. He closed his hand into a fist and let it fall by his side.

Like any wound, the guilt gashing his conscience would scar over in time. And when it did, he would be left with the knowledge that he'd done the right thing. The just thing. The only thing he could live with. ''I know you can't believe me, but I'm going to make things right. Now get your daughter. She needs to look at some pictures while her memory is still fresh. I'll drive you.''

Jacqueline brushed the back of her hand across her cheeks. She raised her eyes and glared at him, her stare cold. ''All right. If that's the way you feel, you give me no choice.'' Spinning on her heel, she marched down the hall and disappeared into her daughter's bedroom.

Dillon stared at the door long after she'd closed it behind her. He'd won this battle, but the win gave him damn little satisfaction. He'd give almost anything to leave the little girl alone and let her and her mama heal, but he couldn't. Soon she would be safe in his office, looking through a photo lineup that included a mug shot of Buck Swain. Mark Schettler would have justice yet, and Mark and Jacqueline's daughter would be safe. Dillon would make sure of it.

He scuffed the leather soles of his boots on the worn hardwood floor and glanced around the Victorian. The air smelled of toast and coffee and the comfort of morning routine. Simple secondhand furniture and a few restored antiques dotted the living room. Dillon knew that when Jacqueline had left her husband she'd taken nothing with her, not a stick of furniture, not one spot of expensive art. From the look of things, she had built a brand-new life for herself and her little girl. A comfortable, well-worn, safe life.

A tabletop weighed down with family pictures stood in front of two lace-dressed windows. Amanda as a red and wrinkled newborn stared googly-eyed from an eight-by-ten. In an adjacent snapshot, her daddy held her on a horsey swing, his face as heart-whole and round as a boy's. That straight-shooting look was long gone by the time his path had crossed Dillon's. Clearly Mark had changed a lot in the past few years.

Dillon reached behind school portraits of Amanda

and picked up a photo of Jacqueline, in hiking boots and a sheepskin coat, perched atop a river bluff. She held her chin high, the wind whipping her hair, her eyes clear and blue as the winding river below.

He ran a finger over the glass. Jacqueline Schettler had a power, a force of will unlike any woman he'd ever met. A force reserved for mama grizzlies and avenging angels. A force to reckon with. Even from the two-dimensional surface of the photograph, that force seemed to reach out and grab him by the throat.

Her force was strongest when she looked at or talked about her little girl. She loved her daughter more than life itself, that had been clear from the first time he'd laid eyes on her. And from that first moment, he'd respected her devotion to family. Hell, he admired it. After all, a deep love for family was the one thing he and Jacqueline had in common.

He set the picture in its spot on the table. Funny how the same thing he admired most about her was now the thing that could stand in his way.

As Jacqueline's footsteps clicked back into the room, he turned away from the photos. She walked past him and into the foyer, Amanda in tow, both wrapped to the gills in winter coats, caps and scarves.

Striding across the living room toward them, he fished in the pocket of his duster for his jangling keys. "My truck is parked out back."

Jacqueline didn't bother to return his gaze. She reached for the knob and flung the door open. "We're not going anywhere with you."

"Where are you going?"

Slowly she turned to face him. Resolve flashed in the depths of those blue, blue eyes. "Thanks to my divorce, I learned the only way to fight legal bluster is with more legal bluster. I'm going to get a lawyer on my side.''

His gut clenched. He should have known she wouldn't give up so easily. He needed her permission to talk to Amanda, and once she talked to a lawyer, she wouldn't allow him within fifty miles of the girl. He closed the space between them in four strides. ''We're both on the same side in this, Jacqueline. We both want to bring the man who killed your ex-husband to justice. We both want to keep Amanda safe.''

''No, Dillon. We're not on the same side. All you *really* want is to bring this man to justice. I have to think about my daughter's safety first.'' Clutching Amanda's hand, she stepped outside, the wind sending her chestnut hair billowing around her face like storm clouds around a lightning rod. ''Lock up before you leave.'' She tossed him one last scowl and slammed the door behind her and her little girl.

He lunged for the door, but stopped himself before he yanked it open. He wanted to run after them. He wanted to throw Jacqueline's wisp of a body over his shoulder, haul her and her daughter into his truck and force them to cooperate. But that was plumb crazy. He couldn't force anything. Not where the law was concerned, and not where Jacqueline's trust was concerned, either.

He raised his eyes to the Victorian's tall ceiling and dragged a hand through his hair. He'd blown his chance. And as a result, he might have blown not only his entire case, but any chance of renewing the connection that he and Jacqueline had once shared.

THE ONCE-PRISTINE snowdrifts framing Spaight Street had decayed into tiny mounds of gray slush. Heavy and moist, the air carried the odor of Lake Monona's early thaw. Cars lining the curb still wore chalky cloaks of crystallized road salt, echoing the color of the sky.

Jacqueline slammed her car door and trudged up the sidewalk to her house, despair seeping into her bones like the cold, drab weather. She clutched Amanda's hand, her daughter dragging despondently by her side. After visiting the three lawyers she knew in the city, she'd found out she couldn't get in to see any of them until this afternoon. She was no closer to knowing what to do than she had been when she'd walked out of the house an hour ago, leaving Dillon standing in the doorway, mouth agape. She almost smiled at the memory. At least by staying away from the house for that long, she could be sure he was gone.

And thank God for that. A shiver clambered up her spine at the memory of his bigger-than-life presence. His black eyes that seemed to peer into her heart. His strong arms that had held her the night the threats began. His smoky drawl that had promised to keep her family safe.

When she first met him she'd believed he was a hero. A white knight dedicated to upholding justice and protecting the innocent. But then the threats had begun. The threats against Mark. Against Amanda. Then she'd seen the real Dillon Reese. And protecting the innocent wasn't nearly as important to him as upholding justice.

She'd tried to hate the man. She'd spent night after

sleepless night cursing the day he was born, but it hadn't done any good. She could blame him for Mark's death, she could blame him for the danger Amanda faced, but somehow she couldn't hate him. He wasn't a bad man, she knew that. He wasn't an evil man. He didn't want to hurt Amanda.

It was worse than that. Much worse.

He truly believed he was doing the right thing. And that was the problem. Doing the right thing was so important to him that he would sacrifice everything, even her little girl, if he had to. Even if he didn't mean to put Amanda at risk, even if he didn't mean to endanger her, the result would be the same.

And it was a result she couldn't live with.

What he would do next, she didn't know, but it didn't really matter. For as much as Dillon loved justice, she loved Amanda more. Amanda wouldn't testify. She wouldn't be one of Dillon's witnesses. She wouldn't follow in her father's footsteps. Jacqueline would make sure of it. She just had to figure out how.

Resolutely she climbed the wooden steps to her front porch, her precious little girl by her side. Except for her disclosure to Dillon, Amanda had barely spoken a word in the past eighteen hours. She had gone through enough trauma to last a lifetime. Jacqueline would give up anything to make sure her baby didn't have to go through any more.

Turning her key in the lock, she heard the faint ring of the telephone inside. Let it ring. It was probably someone from the newspaper looking for an interview with the dead man's ex-wife. Or the district attorney's office checking up on her. She entered the house with Amanda in tow and closed and locked the door behind them.

The phone kept ringing.

She paused and glanced at the white cordless receiver on the kitchen counter. Maybe one of the lawyers' offices was calling. Jacqueline had pleaded with the receptionists to call immediately if they received a cancellation. The sooner Jacqueline could talk to a lawyer, the better. Mustering her courage, she crossed into the kitchen and picked up the phone. "Hello?"

"Jacqueline Schettler?" The low voice grated like a steel-shank boot on wet gravel.

Jacqueline's ears hummed. Her throat grew hot and dry as sunburn. She knew this voice. She recognized... Oh, God.

"Don't say a word. Just listen. Are you listening?"

The acrid taste of fear assaulted her mouth and turned her stomach. The voice on the phone was the same one that had threatened Mark's life. Even though she hadn't heard that voice since her divorce, she'd never forget that low growl. Not as long as she lived.

Buck Swain.

"Are you listening, Jacqueline?"

"Yes," she managed to whisper. She clutched the phone, the plastic slick in her clammy palms. "I'm listening."

"Good. I know your girl was at the brew pub. I know you talked to Dillon Reese this morning. I'm giving you one chance to get out of state. One chance. I don't like the thought of dealing with a child. I'm an honorable man. But I will kill her if you force me to. Do you understand?''

Panic swelled inside her, threatening to erupt in screams. She understood. She understood perfectly. Her head whirled. She leaned against the counter for balance. "Yes, I understand."

"Good. I'll be watching, Jacqueline, so don't call the police and don't try any tricks. If you do, her blood will be on your hands." A click sounded, and the line went dead.

She let the phone slip from her hand, the plastic clattering on the kitchen floor. Her vision blurred. Her knees wobbled. All her fears, all her worst nightmares were coming true.

She pressed her hands to her cheeks, trying to cool her burning skin, trying to clear her spinning head. She needed to think, to focus on some kind of plan. Nausea clamped her stomach. She willed it away. She couldn't give in to panic. Not now. She had to keep her mind sharp. Her daughter's life depended on it—depended on her. The police couldn't help her. Dillon couldn't help her.

She needed to pack her car, raid her meager bank account and drive as fast as she could for the Illinois border. She needed to leave Wisconsin and never come back. Ever. She had to save her little girl. If she didn't— She couldn't let herself think about the alternative.

Chapter Three

Dillon leaned against the doorjamb of District Attorney Neil Fitzroy's office and tried his best to look relaxed. Truth be told, he was anything but. The muscles in his arms and legs coiled with tension like a wildcat ready to spring. He could still see the contempt in Jacqueline's eyes. Still hear her car engine rev to life and pull out into traffic. Still taste the ashen flavor of failure—his steady diet nowadays. Ignoring the others in the room, he zeroed in on the district attorney. "She's getting herself a lawyer, Fitz. Looks like we got a fight on our hands."

Fitz looked up from the sheaf of paper on his desk. From his movie-star face and satin-smooth voice to his talent for hiring good people and delegating with authority, Neil Fitzroy was everything a successful district attorney had to be. His piercing green eyes touched on each of the other three members of his experimental task force on violent crime before latching on to Dillon. "You're sure the little girl saw the murder and can identify the killer? Forcing a child to testify is tricky enough without some witness-rights lawyer in the mix. Is it going to be worth the hassle?''

Again the image of Jacqueline Schettler flashed through Dillon's mind, the lines of tension rimming her mouth and eyes, the stiff, battle-ready carriage of her spine. He was in for a hassle, all right. But if little Amanda could lead him to Buck Swain, it would be worth any hassle Jacqueline could cook up. ''The little girl watched while her daddy was killed. It'll be worth it.''

Fitz's frown deepened. ''We can't afford another mistake on this case, Reese. Buck Swain is a celebrity, a war hero with the scars to prove it. You know how the news media loves that kind of thing. And now a witness dead— Let's not give them any more flub-ups to write about.''

Dillon returned the frown. ''Politicking is your job, Fitz. My job is to win justice.''

Dex Harrington cleared his throat with an annoying coughing growl and pushed his glasses up the bridge of his nose. ''You're right, Fitz, we can't let this case get out of control. Reese sometimes forgets he's not in the wild West anymore. I'll deal with the media on this one. I have the experience and tact to handle them.''

Dillon gritted his teeth. The man probably had calluses from patting his own back. A pretty-boy assistant D.A. with sandy hair and a cleft chin, Harrington wore glasses not to see better but to make himself look more serious and dependable. Two qualities he damn well didn't own.

Dillon opened his mouth to defend himself. Thinking better of it, he snapped it shut. Dex might look like an up-and-comer, but a look was all it was. He had no real power. At least, not while Fitz was still in office. After the next election, things might be different. But for now, Dillon could afford to ignore Dex Harrington.

Next to Dex, Kit Ashner tossed her cropped, mousy hair and shot Dillon one of her conspiratorial looks. "Gee, Dex. Why can't we all be as astute and politically savvy as you?" She rolled her eyes, not bothering to temper her sarcasm. Too busy building her career to suffer fools lightly, Kit was known in the D.A.'s office for her caustic remarks and downright bitchiness. The woman had so many rough edges, Fitz kept her tucked away from the media whenever possible. But personality aside, she worked harder, longer hours than anyone in the office but Dillon himself.

Or maybe Britt Alcott. The classy-looking blonde sitting on the other side of Fitz's desk could pull long hours with the best of them. At least she used to, before her recent marriage. Britt sat straight in her chair, her legs crossed at the ankles, deep concern shining in her blue eyes and wrinkling her fair-skinned brow. "If the little girl witnessed her father's death, you need to be very careful about how you proceed on this, Dillon. You don't want to put extra strain on her. Has anyone looked into getting her psychiatric help to deal with what she saw?"

Dillon nodded in Britt's direction. He hadn't thought about that before. Little Amanda had gone through hell. She would surely need help to handle what she'd witnessed. "Another reason to get her into protective custody."

Fitz's intercom buzzed, halting the conversation. He picked up the phone. "Yes? Send him in." As he dropped the phone back in its cradle, the door swung wide.

Detective Al Mylinski ambled into the room, his mouth twisted into a familiar pucker while he sucked on a piece of his endless stream of fruity candy. "Got some news. News you folks are gonna like." Mylinski slowly, dramatically surveyed the room, nodding to each member of the task force. He reserved one of his lopsided grins for Dillon. "Especially you, Dillon."

Leave it to Mylinski to draw out a story. "Out with it, Al. I've never known you to be tongue-tied."

Mylinski's grin stretched ear to ear. "No, I suppose not. We found ourselves another witness. Seems a bartender at the Schettler Brew Pub was near the kitchen window at the time of the murder. She had a perfect view. Saw everything. Her name is Valerie Wallace."

"Why didn't I hear about her last night?"

"She lied to the cops who interviewed her. Said she didn't see anything. Scared, I guess. But her conscience and my charm finally got the best of her. She's downstairs looking at some pictures as we speak."

Good old Mylinski. Dillon allowed a smile to form on his lips and spread over his face. Another witness. An adult this time. Maybe he wouldn't need little Amanda's testimony in court after all. If he could promise her daughter wouldn't have to testify, maybe Jacqueline would let him arrange for some kind of counseling for the little girl. If the state wouldn't foot the bill, he'd pay for it himself.

Jacqueline's vanilla scent flitted through his mind. The husky quality in her voice echoed in his ear. He'd enjoy taking away the desperate gleam in her eyes, smoothing the lines of tension from her beautiful face. He'd enjoy it more than he cared to think about. "Come on, Al. Introduce me to your bartender. Let's find out exactly what she saw last night."

DILLON BOUNDED UP the wood steps of Jacqueline's old Victorian, Mylinski thumping up the stairs behind him. The interview with the bartender had gone well, better than he had dared hope. Val Wallace had seen the murder and the murderer. It had taken her less than a heartbeat to identify Swain's picture.

Which meant that he didn't need little Amanda Schettler to testify. He didn't try to hold back his smile. It wasn't often that he could give people good news. He couldn't wait to deliver this particular piece to Jacqueline.

He pressed the doorbell button. The light tinkle of chimes jingled through the house. He waited. No movement came from inside. He rapped the oak door with his knuckles, the deep, hollow timbre reverberating off the ceiling and floor of the porch.

Nothing. He looked at his watch. Four hours had passed since Jacqueline had run out of the house to meet with a lawyer. She must still be out. Either that, or she was inside waiting for him to get discouraged and leave. He walked across the porch to one of the narrow windows. She'd have a long wait. She should know by now he didn't give up easily.

The window's antique glass rippled like water, reflecting the overcast sky. He peered through the white lace curtains and into the living room. The room appeared as before. The same tall white walls and wood moldings, the same simple furniture. Everything exactly the same.

Except…

"The pictures. The whole table full of pictures." Adrenaline flooded his system like a jolt of Mylinski's infamous coffee. He spun around and strode down the porch steps toward the car. "Damn. I must have pushed her too hard."

Mylinski jogged behind, his footsteps thundering on the wooden steps. "Not following you. What pictures?"

Dillon opened the sedan's passenger door and ducked inside. Mylinski jumped into the driver's seat. He started the engine and paused, waiting for the punch line.

"The family pictures. She had a whole table full of family pictures. They're gone."

Understanding dawned in Mylinski's shrewd hazel eyes. "Jackie's flown the coop."

"She couldn't have left too long ago. Maybe we can catch her before she gets too far."

"I'm on it," Mylinski said, grabbing for his radio and stepping on the gas.

CLAMPING HER HANDS to the steering wheel, Jacqueline piloted her car up the on-ramp leading to the interstate. She didn't dare review her decision. She didn't dare think about leaving her home, her work, the brew pub her father had built from the ground up. She just drove. She had to reach the Illinois border. It was her only chance to save her little girl.

Two miles passed before she worked up the courage to check the highway behind her. A green sedan followed several car lengths back. A rusted-out truck pulled even with her in the passing lane, its engine roaring above the pounding of her heart.

She held her breath until the truck drove past, then glanced at her daughter. Amanda stared out the window at the snowy winter scenery whizzing by. She squeezed her stuffed horse to her chest.

Guilt chilled Jacqueline to the bone. If only she'd done things differently from the very beginning. Divorcing Mark wasn't enough. She should have moved away, far away, the night she'd received Swain's first threatening phone call. She should have put her daughter's safety first.

If she had, Amanda wouldn't have seen what she'd seen, and she wouldn't be suffering so now. "Sweetheart, everything is going to be okay. We'll go to Chicago, stay in a hotel and visit the museums. We'll have an adventure." Even to Jacqueline the promises sounded as brittle and transparent as fine crystal.

Amanda nodded, clutching Dorsey the Horsey with all her strength as if the stuffed horse was the only thing she could really count on.

Jacqueline riveted her gaze to the road. Soon Amanda would be safe. And that was all that mattered. She checked the mirror again.

Blue and red lights flashed from the roof of the state trooper's car behind her.

No.

She looked down at the speedometer of her car. She couldn't possibly have been going fast enough to catch the state trooper's attention, could she? Had Dillon discovered they were gone and sounded the alarm?

She pulled the car to the shoulder of the interstate and stopped. Her heartbeat throbbed in her head and resonated in her ears. In her side mirror she watched the state trooper climb from his car and walk slowly, deliberately to the driver's window.

She rolled down the window just as he peered inside. Drawing in a deep breath, she prayed she could keep her voice from faltering. "What can I do for you, Officer?" She looked into the trooper's face, her hands shaking so hard she could barely grasp the wheel.

"May I see your driver's license?"

Her heart tumbled into a free fall. If Dillon had discovered her gone, if he was looking for her, the state trooper would know as soon as he picked up his radio.

The man stood waiting, his hand held out for the license. Her face reflected in his sunglasses, distorted and twisted like a reflection in a fun-house mirror. The strong odor of car exhaust heightened the spinning in her head, the rolling of her stomach. What could she do? If she said she didn't have the license, he could easily call in her car's license plate and get the same information. If he hadn't already.

She had to remain cool. She'd just left the house. Maybe Dillon hadn't discovered she was gone yet. Maybe the trooper would write her a speeding ticket and send her on her way. With trembling fingers she pulled her license from her wallet and handed it to him. The trooper ambled back to his car and ducked inside.

Listening to the traffic whiz by on the interstate, she held her breath. Was Swain watching as he'd said he would? He'd warned her against going to the police for help. Would he see her talking to the state trooper and jump to the wrong conclusions? Her stomach balled into a hard knot.

Minute followed minute. Cool air buffeted her face through the open window, the wake of passing cars. She worried her bottom lip between her teeth until it was sore. If only she could stomp her foot on the gas pedal and run. But that would never work. No matter how fast she drove, she could never outrun the state trooper's radio. Anyway, she'd never subject Amanda to the danger of a high-speed chase. She couldn't risk her daughter. Physically or emotionally. Never again.

She found Amanda's hand and enfolded it in hers, whether for her little girl's reassurance or her own, she didn't know.

Finally the trooper emerged from his car. His boots crunched on the gravel, announcing him long before he arrived at her window. He bent at the waist, peering inside. "Mrs. Schettler?"

Her heart lurched at the sound of her name. She looked up into his face, the glistening fear in her eyes reflected in his sunglasses. She forced her voice to function. "Yes?"

"I'm going to have to ask you to come with me. The D.A. is looking for you."

Jacqueline closed her eyes, the horror of his words rushing through her veins and paralyzing her heart. She couldn't think. She couldn't move. All she could do was clutch Amanda's warm little hand.

Swain had given her one chance to get out of state. One chance. And now that chance was gone.

DILLON'S OFFICE WAS far smaller than Jacqueline remembered. Stacks of paper covered every available surface. Its bland, government-beige walls seemed to close in with every breath she took. Focusing on the battered desk, she cuddled Amanda on her lap and willed away the unbearable dizziness that had intensified during the ride in the state trooper's car.

The door swung wide and Dillon himself walked into the office, his long-legged, rolling stride like that of a sheriff busting into the local saloon. The small office grew even smaller, the stuffy air stuffier. This whole building wasn't big enough to house a man like Dillon Reese, let alone this cramped little office. He belonged in worn blue jeans on the open range, not here in a glorified cubicle dressed in suit and tie.

He studied her for a moment through squinted black eyes before he nodded. "Jacqueline."

She shifted on the crackling vinyl upholstery of her chair and hugged Amanda close, taking some comfort from the soft warmth of her daughter's little body and the scent of no-tears shampoo. "Why did you drag us down here? What do you want now?"

"I have good news." His deep, smoky voice filled every nook of the room. He sauntered over to his desk, snakeskin boots thudding on the low carpet. Leaning a hip on the worn desktop, he watched her, his lips stretching into a grin. A devastatingly handsome grin.

Something inside her squirmed. She couldn't let herself trust that smile. He had manipulated her before by flashing his white teeth. He'd promised her good news before when he couldn't deliver. She had no reason to believe anything was different now. "We don't have the same definition of good, Dillon."

His smile seemed to widen, and she could swear a twinkle materialized in his black eyes. "We found another witness. An adult. We can make our case without Amanda."

She let his words seep into her like raindrops after a long drought, not sure how she should respond. Suspicion tugged at the corners of her mind. "So why did you haul us down here?"

"I want to talk to you about setting up some counseling sessions to help Amanda deal with what she saw. That's all. Her role in this case is finished." He slid a thigh onto the desk and watched for Jacqueline's response as if he'd just given her a precious and unexpected gift.

He probably believed he had. If he had said those same words this morning, she might have believed it, too.

But Swain's voice on the telephone had changed all that. Echoes of his guttural growl had shaken what hope she had left loose from its moorings. He'd given her one chance to keep Amanda safe, and that chance was gone. It was too late for Dillon's promises. Much too late. All the promises in the world couldn't help her daughter now. Her only chance was to make a dash for the Illinois border. Even now she might be able to make it before Swain caught up with her. It was a long shot, but it was the only shot she had.

She took a deep breath of stuffy air and willed herself to remain calm. "I'm not interested."

Staring at her as if she'd spoken another language, he raked a big hand through the waves of his black hair. "I don't think you understand me."

"I understand you perfectly." She slid Amanda off her lap, stood up and held her daughter's hand. "I'll deal with the problem on my own. There are plenty of qualified child psychologists out there. I don't need you to set up anything."

He frowned and paused as if struggling to come to terms with her rejection. "All right. Whatever you want. But I'm going to arrange for an officer to be posted outside your door until Swain is brought in. Just to be safe."

Raising her chin, she met his black eyes and didn't flinch. "You go right ahead and do that. Goodbye, Dillon."

A forceful knock on the door nearly startled her off her feet.

Dillon turned his frustrated frown on the door. "Come in."

Detective Mylinski burst into the room, a fine sheen of sweat on his brow. He looked exactly the same as he had when she'd seen him last, as if his balding head hadn't lost even one hair, his paunchy belly hadn't gained even one pound. But she'd never seen the detective upset before. His pudgy face was flushed, his eyes more bugged out than usual. Opening his mouth to speak, he froze when he spotted Jacqueline. "Can I talk to you, Dillon?"

Dillon's black gaze flicked to Jacqueline, then back to the detective. "Can it wait a minute, Al?"

The detective shook his head. "I think you'll want to hear this now."

A prick of dread propelled Jacqueline's pulse into overdrive. Fear rose in her chest. Something had happened, something he didn't want her to hear. "What is it? What happened?"

Stone-faced, the detective stared pointedly at Dillon. "In private."

"Will she find out sooner or later?" Dillon asked.

Detective Mylinski nodded reluctantly.

"Then out with it."

Mylinski folded his arms over his belly. He looked down at Amanda.

Catching his reluctance to speak in front of her daughter, Jacqueline followed his gaze. Amanda's blue eyes reflected the fear that coiled around Jacqueline's heart.

Dillon crossed the room in three strides and threw open the door. He leaned out into the hallway.

"Britt? Would you mind keeping an eye on a little girl for a minute?"

A blond woman entered the doorway. "No problem. She can come over to my office." She gestured to an even smaller room directly across the hall.

Amanda clutched Jacqueline's hand as if she'd never let go. Jacqueline didn't want to let her little girl out of her grasp either, even for a second. But she had to know what had happened. From Mylinski's demeanor, she'd bet a lot of money it was something horrible. And it had something to do with Amanda. She knelt beside her daughter. "Go ahead, punkin. We'll leave the doors open so you can see me the whole time."

"That's a great idea," the blonde said cheerily, holding out her hand to Amanda.

Slowly Amanda let go of Jacqueline's hand and clutched Dorsey the Horsey with both arms. Ignoring the woman's outstretched hand, she dragged her feet across the hall to the other room, never taking her gaze from Jacqueline for more than two steps.

Once her daughter was safely sequestered in the other office, Jacqueline focused on Mylinski. She pressed her arms against her sides to keep her hands from shaking. "What happened?"

Dillon nodded to the detective.

"It's about our other witness. The bartender, Val Wallace."

Val? Jacqueline knew Val. The voluptuous blonde had tended bar at the pub for at least five years, an almost unprecedented length of time in an industry that saw staggering employee turnover. On the outside, Val was as hardened as a streetwalker. But on the inside, she could be sweeter than Mary Poppins, especially where Amanda was concerned. Jacqueline had always liked Val.

Dillon stepped away from the door, his boot heels striking the floor with a sharp thud. Black eyes narrowing on the detective, he moved behind his desk. "What about Val? Is she going back on her story?"

Detective Mylinski slowly shook his balding head. "She's dead."

Chapter Four

Dillon slammed his fist on the paper-strewn surface of his desk. The sting of the blow shot up his arm. He'd promised Val protection. And now, like Mark, she was dead.

He could sense Jacqueline Schettler beside him. She didn't move a muscle. She scarcely seemed to breathe.

He didn't look at her. He couldn't. He didn't want to see the bone-deep fear and grief he knew would be wrenching her beautiful face. He didn't want to see the blame chilling her blue eyes. He couldn't face those things now. Not yet. Not until he had some answers. Not until he knew what he was going to do next.

He focused instead on Mylinski. His friend returned his scrutiny, mirroring the anger and guilt Dillon knew haunted his own eyes. "How the hell did this happen, Al? She was in protective custody, for God's sake. Where was her protection?"

Mylinski held up his hands in a calming motion. Red faced and sweating, he looked as if he was ripe for a heart attack. "There was nothing Dale Kearney could do."

Dillon forced himself to think calmly. He knew Dale Kearney. He'd worked with the red-haired detective many times over the years. A former military officer, Kearney was a good cop. A thorough cop. Not given to making stupid mistakes. But the need for an explanation, the need to fix blame, the need to end the killing hacked at his nerves like a dull hatchet. "How was she killed? Who knew where she was? I want answers, damn it."

"She was walking from Kearney's car to the apartment we arranged for her to stay in. The killer had a high-powered rifle. Two shots to the head."

Dillon had done countless hours of research in preparation for Swain's trial. He knew Buck Swain inside and out. Certainly well enough to know the snake was as comfortable with a high-powered rifle in his hands as a cowhand was with a branding iron. "Swain was a member of special forces in the army. A sniper in the Green Berets. Where was he when he took the shots?"

"There's a patch of woods next to the apartment complex. We're sweeping the area now. So far we haven't found any witnesses or evid—"

A slight sound, like the gentle whisper of wind, cut through Mylinski's explanation. Almost against his will, Dillon turned to look at Jacqueline.

She stared straight ahead, her gaze riveted on her little girl in the office across the hall. She uttered the sound again. "I can't lose her. Please, let us go."

"I won't let anything happen to her. She'll be safe, I give you my word." The moment the words left his lips, he recognized how lame his promise sounded. As Jacqueline had pointed out to him before, he hadn't been able to protect Mark.

And now Val.

Jacqueline looked up at him. Desperation shone from her eyes. "Please."

"Swain knew where to find Mark. He knew where to find Val. He'll find you, too."

"If I can get Amanda across state lines, he'll leave us alone."

"And what in God's name makes you think that?"

"He said he would."

Her declaration hit Dillon in the gut like an iron fist. Swain had contacted her. The events of the past few hours shifted into place in his mind. "You weren't running from me this afternoon. You were running from Swain."

She nodded weakly.

He fought to keep himself from pounding the desktop until his fist was bloody. "And he gave you instructions not to contact me or the police, didn't he?"

She nodded again. "He said he'd kill—" She pressed her fingers over her mouth as if the words were too horrible to say aloud. Her eyes filled with moisture. "Please let us go."

"Even if you believed him at first, what makes you think he'll give you the chance to get across the border now that you've been sitting in my office for the last thirty minutes? What makes you think he'll stop at the border?"

She met his eyes, hers desperate, almost hopeless. From her look he could tell she'd asked herself this question countless times since the state trooper had escorted her here. And she'd come up with the same answer he had. "I have to believe something. It's the only chance we have."

How could he argue with her? He'd love to be able to tell her that the system wouldn't let her down. Not as it had let Mark down. Not as it had let Val down. But it would be a waste of breath. She would never believe him. Even he didn't believe it anymore.

Buck Swain had been ahead of the system at every turn. He'd known every move Dillon made before he made it. As soon as Dillon had identified Valerie Wallace as a witness, Swain had silenced her. After Dillon had left the Schettler house, Swain had threatened Jacqueline. "Your phone number—it's unlisted. Who have you given the number to?"

Jacqueline thought for a moment. "Amanda's school, my work, your office of course, Mark, my mother in Germany…. I left my number with a couple of lawyers' offices this morning. That's about it, I guess. No one else knows it."

"Except Buck Swain."

She shivered slightly. Taking a deep breath, she raised her chin and seemed to will the fear from her eyes. "He's watching us."

"What else did he say?"

"He knew Amanda was at the pub last night. He knew about your visit this morning."

A picture took shape in Dillon's mind. A damn ugly picture. A picture that tightened his throat and drew his hands into fists. His gut roiled with futility, betrayal, nail-spitting anger. "Someone is feeding him the information."

Mylinski's eyes honed to points. "What are you thinking, Dillon?" He leaned toward Dillon and Jacqueline, his voice low as a whisper.

Dillon kept his voice equally low. If this hunch was right, he, too, didn't want anyone around the office to pick up wisps of their conversation. "I want a list of everyone who knew that Amanda and Val Wallace witnessed Mark's murder. Everyone."

"That's easy. Hardly anyone knew. Just Fitzroy's task force, Kearney and me." Mylinski paused for less than a second. "You think someone in the D.A.'s office or the sheriff's department is leaking information to Swain, don't you?"

It was exactly what he was thinking, but hearing Mylinski say the words out loud infused him with a fresh surge of rage. "It would explain a lot. I'm not taking any chances." He glanced from Jacqueline to her daughter and back again. He'd lost two witnesses. He would *not* lose these two.

As if feeling the direction of his thoughts, Jacqueline looked up into his eyes, chin raised, back straight, tough as rawhide. But there was something vulnerable under the brave surface. Something that had reached into him from the first time he'd met her and had grasped hold of his heart. Something he couldn't, wouldn't let down.

Jacqueline and her daughter needed someone to go the extra mile to protect them, and he was the one.

He circled the desk and gently cupped her elbow in the palm of his hand. "I'll get to the bottom of this, Jacqueline. I'll find out who is feeding Swain information. I know you have no reason to believe me, but I *will* protect you and Amanda. I won't rely on the D.A.'s office or the police. I'll do it myself this time. I'm the only one who will know where you are. Nothing is going to happen to your little girl. Swain will have to kill me first.''

Panic rose in Jacqueline's throat. More death. More promises. She had to get Amanda out of here. Away from the district attorney's offices. Away from Swain's informant. Away from the danger.

But how?

If Dillon was right and Swain had eyes and ears in the district attorney's offices, he'd already know she was here. And he'd be waiting for her to leave. Waiting to kill Amanda.

She met Dillon's black eyes. He'd promised he would protect Amanda personally. He'd sworn he would shield her with his life.

Could he keep his promise this time? Would it be enough?

She could only hope and pray. Because as much as she hated to admit it, the man she'd sworn she'd never trust again appeared to be her best bet. Her only bet. ''Please. Get us out of here.''

Dillon gave her a curt nod and turned to Detective Mylinski. ''We need a decoy, Al.''

The detective screwed up his shiny forehead in thought. ''I'll call downstairs and get a female officer up here to stand in for Jacqueline.''

''No good. It would involve too many people. The fewer who know about this, the better.'' Dillon spun toward the door. His gaze latched on to the blond woman hovering over Amanda. ''Britt? Would you come in here, please? And bring Amanda.''

Amanda shot from her chair as if spring-loaded,

scampered across the hallway and leapt into Jacqueline's arms.

Jacqueline enfolded her and hugged her close. She leaned her cheek against her daughter's silken head and breathed in her scent. Her little girl. Her baby. A shiver slithered over her skin as if a dozen covert eyes were watching them. She held her daughter tighter. She had to get Amanda somewhere she would be safe. They had to get out of the district attorney's office.

Britt followed Amanda, Mylinski swinging the door shut behind her. "Dillon?"

"We need you to go with Al. To pose as Jacqueline. We need you to be a decoy."

Britt's ice-blue gaze flitted over Jacqueline and Amanda. "How dangerous is this going to be?"

"Dangerous. I can't lie to you. But we'll take precautions. And I doubt we'll fool our man for long. I just need you to distract him long enough to allow me to get Jacqueline and Amanda out of here. I'm sorry I can't tell you more."

Britt raised her chin and nodded to Dillon. "Do you want me to switch clothing?"

"No. Just cover your hair. We want him to think you're Jacqueline for only a few minutes. I don't want him taking shots at you."

"That wouldn't be my preference, either." She gave Jacqueline and Amanda a little smile. "You're in good hands with Dillon, you know. He'll take care of everything."

Jacqueline nodded in response. God, she hoped the willowy blonde was right. Because he was her only chance. Amanda's only chance.

Dillon spun on his heel and strode to his desk. Yanking open a bottom drawer, he pulled out a small laundry bag stuffed to the brim with wrinkled white shirts.

Mylinski frowned. "You still living in your office?"

"I'm not doing your laundry, Dillon." Britt shook her head. "That's where I draw the line."

Dillon focused on Jacqueline. "Does Amanda have a hat?"

Jacqueline reached into the pocket of Amanda's coat and produced her knitted pink hat with the pom-pon on top.

Dillon crossed the office to her, plucked the hat from her hand and perched it on top of the laundry bag. "Britt? Do you still have that knitted blanket in your office?"

"Sure do." She ducked out the door. When she returned, she wore a gray coat and her own stocking cap jammed down to conceal every wisp of blond hair. She held out a blue-and-white afghan to Dillon.

Settling the laundry bag in Britt's arms, Dillon draped the afghan over it. If Jacqueline hadn't seen him construct the disguise, she might well believe Britt had a sleeping child snuggled against her shoulder.

"Al will drive you to the sheriff's training center near Waunakee. Before you get out of the car, get rid of the laundry bag and take off that hat. I don't want you taking any unnecessary chances."

When the door closed behind Britt Alcott and the detective, Dillon once again turned his razor-sharp gaze on Jacqueline. "We may not have a very big window of opportunity here. Are you ready?"

Ready? She'd been ready since before she'd set foot in this office. She propped Amanda on her hip and hugged her close. "Just get us out of here."

"Do you want me to carry Amanda? We have quite a ways to go. She might get a little heavy for you."

Amanda buried her face in Jacqueline's neck and clung.

"It's okay, punkin." Jacqueline kissed her little ear. "I'm used to carrying her. I'll be fine. Just lead the way."

He nodded and moved to the door, Jacqueline and Amanda on his heels. After pausing to listen for a moment, he opened the door.

"Dillon, you're just the man I want to see," a voice boomed from down the hall. A well-dressed man with sandy hair and glasses strode toward them.

Jacqueline jumped back into the office and ducked behind the door, hugging Amanda close. She gasped for breath. Had he seen them?

Dillon reached in and pulled the office door closed. His muffled voice filtered through the wood. "What do you want, Harrington?"

Jacqueline pressed her ear to the door.

"I hear a state trooper brought Jacqueline Schettler and her daughter in," the forceful voice answered. "I want to talk to the little girl."

"This is my case, Harrington."

"It's the task force's case."

"The task force be damned. The case is mine. Now back off."

"Just doing my job, Reese. Now get out of my way." The doorknob turned.

Jacqueline's breath lodged in her throat. Her heart seemed to stop its rapid tattoo.

"You're too late, Harrington. Detective Mylinski just left with Mrs. Schettler and her daughter."

The doorknob halted in midtwist. "Mylinski? Where is he taking them?"

"To a safe house."

The doorknob returned to its original position. Jacqueline dragged a breath into her starving lungs.

"I'm not going to sit back and let you and Fitz control this case, Reese. Not anymore. I'm going to be looking over your shoulder at every step. This time the case is going to be handled the right way. The way it should have been handled all along."

"Keep your speeches for the campaign trail. You're going to need every ounce of political hot air you have if you run against Fitz," Dillon's voice growled, low and menacing. "Now get the hell out of here. I have work to do."

Jacqueline held her breath. Silence echoed through the hall. Finally the knob twisted again and the door inched open. Dillon's tousled hair and dark eyes peeked into the office. "All clear. Let's go."

Grabbing a deep breath, Jacqueline followed him down the hall and through the austere reception area of the district attorney's offices. They stepped out into the main hallway. The beige tile gleamed faintly in the fluorescent lights buzzing overhead. They passed several steel doors marked Crime Laboratory. Jacqueline tried not to think about the tests conducted in those rooms. Tests on Mark's clothing and the bullets that killed Val.

Ahead of her, Dillon opened one side of a double steel door and ushered them into the lobby. Their shoes clicked on the polished black marble floor. Loud as gunshots. Jacqueline cringed with each step.

Dillon led them to a door marked Stairs, pulled a key from his pocket and slid it into the lock. The clack of the turning mechanism bounced off marble floors and walls. He pushed the door open, and Jacqueline scurried into the stairwell after him.

They plunged ahead, down the stairs. Each footfall echoed off the cement steps. Large pipes cast eerie shadows on the concrete walls. Jacqueline held Amanda tightly to her hip with one hand and gripped the handrail with the other. A numbing chill emanated from the steel rail.

A sound followed them from the stairway above. Very faint. A light scratching noise. A key turning in a lock? Shuffling footsteps? Jacqueline bit her lower lip. The thundering of her own heart drowned out the sound.

In front of her, Dillon paused. He glanced up the stairs, in the direction of the sound, his face an expressionless mask. Reaching back, he grasped her hand in his. Strong, warm.

She held on.

The sound grew louder and then suddenly stopped. Jacqueline followed Dillon's gaze to the large pipes overhead. The sound must be coming from the pipes.

They continued down the stairs. One flight after another. Finally they reached the main floor.

Still holding her hand, he led her through a maze

of halls, out a small side door and into the night. The cold air slapped her cheeks and stole her breath.

He hurried them toward a black truck. Pressing a button on a small remote control, he unlocked the vehicle's doors, yanked open the driver's door and tilted the seat forward. "Lie down on the floor in the back," he said, his tone leaving no opening for questions.

Jacqueline climbed in and lay still as death in the back seat of Dillon's pickup, her arms wrapped tightly around Amanda. Dillon swung himself into the front seat. The truck growled to life and started to move.

Bands of light crept across the interior of the car, plunging them from light to shadow and back again. Amanda curled in her arms, her body tense, her breathing irregular. Jacqueline held her daughter tighter, as if by sheer will she could calm them both. Keep them both safe. But after what she'd heard in Dillon's office, she doubted her little girl would ever be safe again.

The sounds of street traffic faded. The bands of light grew farther and farther apart. The darkness outside the window closed in, thick and black, broken only by the soft glow of the nearly full moon.

Still they drove on.

The events of the past few hours spilled through Jacqueline's mind. Could Dillon be right? Could there be a leak in the district attorney's office or police department? A leak that had led to Mark's and Val's deaths?

She shivered. She'd grown up believing the authorities were the good guys. They protected people and kept her neighborhood safe. She'd taught Amanda to believe the same, taking her to the park where police officers handed out Brewers baseball cards to children and taught them about bicycle safety. Had the world she knew—the world she wanted her daughter to know—changed so much?

She pressed her cheek against the silk of her daughter's hair and drew in the fragrance of her shampoo. An ordinary scent. A comforting scent. A scent from the life they'd left behind. A life that was gone forever.

Raising her face slightly, she focused on the driver's seat. From this angle she could see nothing but the back of Dillon's head, his short, dark waves above the headrest.

He'd gotten them out of the office without anyone seeing them. He'd kept that particular promise. But where did that leave them? Could she trust him to keep her little girl safe?

She had to. Because at this point, she had nowhere else to turn.

Finally the truck rumbled to a stop. Jacqueline lifted her head from the seat, her neck stiff from her awkward position. The moon shed a soft glow on the treetops visible through the truck's windows.

Dillon opened the door and swung from the truck in one motion. "I'm going to have a look around. I'll be back in a second. Stay low in the seat." He slammed the door, and his footsteps faded into the quiet of the night.

Jacqueline cradled Amanda closer.

"Is he going to keep us safe?" Her daughter's voice was nothing more than a faint peep.

Jacqueline hesitated, but only for a moment. "Yes. He'll keep us safe, baby." *He had to.*

Amanda nodded her little head, but said nothing.

The back door opened. Cold air suffused the warm cocoon of the truck's interior.

He held out a hand to help her out. "All clear. Follow me."

She looked at his offered hand. In the stairwell his hand clasping hers had made her feel protected. It had given her a false sense of security. But as much as she wanted to, she couldn't hide behind that sense of security now. She could rely on Dillon to protect them—she had no choice in that—but she needed to be on her toes, as well. She needed to face reality.

Without accepting his hand, she struggled out of the truck, carrying Amanda with her. The image of Buck Swain with a rifle hung on the edge of her mind. She dashed into the open door of an ordinary-looking ranch-style home, Dillon hard on her heels.

The moment Jacqueline set foot in the kitchen, it was clear exactly how *un*ordinary this house was. Stacks of paper and file folders covered every inch of the kitchen table and piled on the countertops. Time-line charts and gruesome photographs were tacked to the walls in the way teenagers decorate their rooms with posters and magazine covers.

Looking past Dillon and into the living room, Jacqueline could see that the file, chart and photograph decor extended to that room, as well. To top it off, a large desk dominated the adjoining room, dwarfing the normal living-room furnishings. The place looked more like a crime task force's war room than a home. So this was what a safe house looked like.

Dillon didn't even glance at the surroundings. He strode across the kitchen floor and opened the refrigerator door. "I'll put together some sandwiches. The two of you must be starving. The bathroom is around the corner if you want to wash up. The bedroom is next to it. You'll be sleeping in there."

"There's only one bedroom?"

"Only one furnished with a bed. I'm the only one who lives here."

Surprise stiffened Jacqueline's spine. "This is *your* house?"

He glanced around the kitchen as if looking for the reason behind her reaction. His brow furrowed with puzzlement, he shifted his focus back to her. "Yes."

She let her gaze roam around the house again. The stacks of file folders, the charts and the pictures. Even down to the cluttered desk, the place looked like a copy of his office downtown.

A chill crept over Jacqueline's skin and delved into her bones. She'd known he was dedicated to his job, to the never-ending fight for justice. She'd known he cared deeply about doing the right thing. But this—the desk, the charts, the photographs—this went far beyond normal dedication. This was obsession. Dillon Reese wasn't just dedicated to winning justice. He was on a crusade.

She looked back at him. "Why did you bring us to your home?"

He focused on the contents of the refrigerator, the sharp planes of his profile illuminated by the refrigerator's light. "No one will ever think to look here. You'll be safe."

Safe.

She glanced down at Amanda once again, at her little girl's tired eyes, glassy and wide with fear. God, Jacqueline wanted to believe they were safe. She ached to believe it.

But could she with a murderer and an informant out there she knew nothing about and a man protecting them who was on his own personal crusade?

She once again allowed her gaze to travel over the papers and photos. Two things were clear. There was more to this case than Dillon was telling her. And there was more driving him than a simple dedication.

She had a lot of questions for the cowboy assistant district attorney. And if she was going to keep her baby safe, she needed answers.

Dillon watched Jacqueline usher her little girl down the hall and disappear into the bathroom. A strange feeling sneaked over him. No one but him had set foot in his house since the day he'd bought this secluded hideaway. And even in his wildest fantasies he'd never imagined Jacqueline living under his roof with him. Eating a meal in his kitchen, taking a shower in his bathroom, sleeping in his bed.

Blood pooled in his groin at the images that popped into his mind. Jacqueline in his shower, water sluicing intimately over her soft, naked curves. Jacqueline in his bed, her long legs tangled in his dark sheets, her chestnut hair fanned out on his pillow.

He raked a hand through his hair and pushed the images from his mind. The circumstances were not the stuff of fantasy. He was hiding Jacqueline's little girl from a murderer, not playing house.

He glanced around the kitchen, his gaze landing on the crime-scene photos tacked to the walls, gruesome in their unblinking detail. Not suitable for a child's eyes. Not suitable at all. Abandoning his sandwich fixings, he turned his attention to clearing the walls.

What else did he need to do to make the house suitable for Jacqueline and her daughter? Pulling pins and stacking photos, he scrolled through a mental checklist. In addition to sandwich fixings, he had eggs and coffee in the refrigerator. That took care of breakfast tomorrow. But after that, he would need to pick up some groceries. Thankfully the sheets on his bed were relatively clean. Toys for Amanda? Maybe he could swing by a toy store tomorrow, too. What kinds of toys did a seven-year-old girl like to play with?

He'd better ask Jacqueline. When it came to trusting him, she was as skittish as a day-old colt. Especially where her daughter was concerned. Understandable after what they'd been through. What he had put her through.

Damn. His blood boiled at the thought of someone in the D.A.'s office or police department leaking the task force's every move to Swain. He'd find the snake responsible. He'd protect Jacqueline and her little girl. After all, he'd promised her. And he'd be damned if he didn't come through this time.

Chapter Five

"I want to know what's going on." Jacqueline stopped just inside the living room, hands on hips. It had taken her over an hour to lull Amanda to sleep. Over an hour she'd stewed her questions over in her mind while she rubbed her daughter's tense little back. Questions about the task force. Questions about Dillon's obvious obsession. And now, when the time had come to deliver her well-thought-out queries, she'd blurted out the first thing that came to her lips.

Hunched behind the desk, shirtsleeves rolled up to his elbows, Dillon looked up from the legal folder spread open in front of him. His tie hung loose around his open shirt collar, a glimpse of dark chest hair peeking through the frame of starched white fabric. As he straightened in the desk chair, his shirt outlined his muscular chest.

She tore her attention from his chest and narrowed her gaze on his eyes. She wanted answers.

He snapped the file folder closed and met her gaze. "I thought I explained everything in my office. I believe there might be a leak in the district attorney's office or police department, so—"

"No." Jacqueline set her chin. Now that Amanda wasn't looking on, she wasn't about to swallow his pat little explanations. "I mean everything. From the beginning. I want to know about each person you think might be giving Swain information."

"This is an official murder investigation and prosecution, Jacqueline. I can't talk about this with you."

She stepped toward him. She'd expected him to give her an answer like this, and she was prepared. "It stopped being official when you decided to cut yourself off from the district attorney's office and smuggle us to your home."

A muscle twitching along his jaw, he stared at her for what seemed like an eternity. His eyes searched, prodded, fierce and intimate at the same time.

The room grew hot. She fought the urge to squirm under his gaze. Taking a deep breath, she held her hands out at her sides, palms up, an entreaty for fairness. "Listen, you've asked me to cooperate with your plan, and I have so far. But I can't do it blindly. If I'm going to do what's best for my daughter, I have to know what's really going on."

He pushed his chair back from the desk. Heaving a resigned sigh, he motioned to a tawny couch tucked in the corner behind the desk. "Why don't you sit down? This could get long."

Jacqueline exhaled with relief. Until he'd spoken, she hadn't realized she was holding her breath. Pressing her lips together, she walked around the desk in the direction of the couch. She perched on the edge of the firm, almost-new upholstery.

He spun his desk chair to face her, his back to the desk. Close enough for her to smell the clean, masculine scent of him. Close enough to feel his body heat. "What do you want to know?"

She drew a deep breath into her hungry lungs. Swallowing hard, she tried to ignore his gaping shirt and the soft-looking dark hair sprinkling his chest and organize the questions bouncing around in her mind. She forced herself to focus on the questions she needed to ask, the answers she needed to hear. "For starters, what is this task force you and the detective were referring to?"

"More populated counties usually have a homicide division or a violent crime division of the district attorney's office. But thankfully, we don't have enough violent crime in Dane County to justify a separate unit. So we have an informal group of experienced assistant district attorneys and investigators who specialize in different areas and work together to prosecute crimes such as armed robbery, rape and murder. The task-force label is merely a political thing. Fitz wants the public to know he's tough on violent crime."

"And you think one of these assistants may be telling Swain everything the group is doing?"

He grimaced as if in pain. "That's what I think." Obviously the idea was a tough one for him to accept.

"What would an assistant D.A. have to gain by doing something like that?"

"Political position, bribe money—it could be any number of things."

"Who is on the task force?"

"Myself, Britt Alcott, Dex Harrington and Kit Ashner."

Alarm seized her chest, making it hard to breathe. "Britt? The blonde? Wasn't she the woman who took Amanda to her office?" Horrible images of Amanda in the clutches of the woman responsible for Mark's and Val's deaths invaded Jacqueline's mind. She forced herself to remain seated on the couch.

Dillon shook his head. "Britt wouldn't have anything to do with Swain," he said, his drawl calm, confident, soothing. "I wouldn't have involved her if I suspected her."

She tried to believe his assurances, but her heart still thumped in her ears. "If not Britt Alcott, who *do* you suspect?"

"It could be anyone else on the task force or the detectives on the case. But I'm betting my money on Dex Harrington or Kit Ashner."

Harrington. The man they'd run into while they were trying to sneak out of Dillon's office. The man who'd insisted on questioning Amanda. "Let's start with Dex Harrington."

Dillon nodded, a look of dislike stealing over his taut features. "Rumor has it that Harrington fancies himself Neil Fitzroy's chief opposition in the coming election for D.A. He would love to discredit Neil and myself in a big case like this."

Jacqueline could barely believe her ears. "Enough to cause two people to be murdered?"

He shot her a you-wanted-to-know look. "Not very pretty, is it? About a year ago I had a case against an armed robber. A prominent citizen had been robbed, so Fitz was under a lot of pressure from the press and the powers that be. My case was weaker than a newborn calf, but I had the defendant believing I could put him away. He was about to deal. That was before he learned just how flimsy our case was. Needless to say, we lost. Last month the snake was arrested for armed robbery and murder in Chicago.''

''And Dex Harrington was the person who told him your case was weak?''

''Dex isn't stupid. He covers his tracks well. I can't prove it, but it had to be him. He's the only one besides Fitz and me who knew enough about the case.'' Dillon's eyes hardened, his voice sharpened with contempt.

She had no doubt that if this were the Old West, Dillon wouldn't wait for a noose to be lowered around a criminal's neck. He'd dispense six-gun justice the moment the guilty verdict was read. ''Can't Fitzroy fire Harrington?''

''Not without justification. Besides, Fitz doesn't want to deal with the kind of political fallout Harrington could cause.''

''Can't you just avoid telling him anything important?''

''I could if he was the only possible leak. But there's Kit.''

Jacqueline made a mental note. ''Another assistant district attorney?''

''Right. She's a damn good lawyer, but her public relations skills leave a lot to be desired.''

Jacqueline definitely wasn't following him. ''Why does that make you suspect her?''

''Fitz doesn't like her to grant interviews with the press. He's afraid she'll make him look bad, so he keeps her away from the high-profile cases. The cases that lead to career growth. And as an ambitious lawyer, Kit is a little bitter.''

''So you think she might be trying to get back at Fitzroy?''

He shrugged, his shoulders rigid. ''She can be pretty ruthless when she wants to be. I don't know if she would go so far as to cause someone's death, but I certainly can't rule it out.''

Jacqueline shook her head. Is that what justice was all about? Political ambition? Had two people been murdered because of one of these lawyers' ambitions? Did her child's life depend on someone's hunger for power? The idea made her sick.

An uncomfortable thought niggled at the back of her mind. All the players in this sick game seemed to have their own agenda. She knew Dillon did. There was no doubt in her mind he felt guilty about his failure to protect Mark. And well he should. But that wasn't reason enough to bring them to his home, to vow to lay down his life to keep them safe. And it wasn't reason to explain why he'd turned his house into an anticrime war room nor his life into a crusade. There was something else going on here. And she needed to find out what. She narrowed her eyes on Dillon. ''How about you? Do you have political ambitions?''

His dark brows arched with surprise. ''Me? I'm about as political as a peeled rattler.''

''Then why are you doing this?''

''This?''

''Bringing us to your home. Vowing to protect Amanda with your life. It seems everyone in your office is motivated by the prospect of political power. What motivates you?''

His eyes darkened. His brows pulled together. ''I want to get murderers off the streets.''

A tiny chill worked its way along her nerves. ''That sounds like a political spiel if I ever heard one.''

He leaned toward her, gripping the arms of his chair. ''I'll get Swain. He won't hurt your little girl. He won't hurt anyone ever again.'' His voice dropped an octave, vengeance echoing in his words.

The chill grew. Uneasiness tightened in the pit of her stomach. Vengeance? Was that what Dillon was after? ''Did Swain do something to you? To someone you loved? If you're using Amanda for some kind of personal crusade, I want to know.''

''No. Swain has never done anything to me personally.''

''But you've turned your home into an office, and you'll risk your life to protect a witness? That's what you promised me. You said you'd protect Amanda with your life.''

He nodded, resolute, the muscles in his jaw tight as piano wire. ''And I aim to keep that promise.''

''Why? Why is this crusade you're on so important?''

He gritted his teeth. The lines of tension around his eyes and mouth deepened. ''A crusade. I guess that's what it is, isn't it?''

''Why is it so important?''

He didn't answer. Instead he reached into his back pocket and pulled out his wallet. Opening it, he plucked out a small photo and handed it to Jacqueline.

She took the photograph from his hand and turned it to the light.

A girl grinned from the picture. Wavy dark hair wisped around her oval face, framing her delicate features like smoke on a windless day. Her skin was smooth as ivory with the unmistakable bloom of youth.

But the thing most noteworthy about her was her smile. Sparkling. Full of life, joy and unquenchable curiosity.

"Who is she?"

His lips hardened. "My little sister. Janey."

Yes, she could see the resemblance. The chiseled cheekbones. The wavy hair. But most of all the eyes. Their eyes had a penetrating quality, as if they could see right through a person's defenses and into her soul. "You look a lot alike."

Dillon nodded.

A niggle of trepidation shimmied up her spine. "You're from Texas, right? Does she live in Texas? Do you see her often?"

He said nothing, his features hard, unreadable.

Foreboding tightened her throat. She forced the question from her lips. "Something happened to her, didn't it?"

"Yes."

"When?"

"Ten years ago."

"What happened?"

He was silent for a long time. Nothing broke the stillness of the room except the quiet ticking of a

clock on the wall. Not a word from his lips. Not a
movement. Just when she thought he wasn't going
to answer, he drew in a deep breath.

"I was just out of law school when Janey decided
she wanted to go away to college." His voice rumbled in the still room like approaching thunder. "My
daddy was dead by then, and Mama was set against
Janey leaving home so young. Hated the idea of her
being so far away in a strange city."

Jacqueline leaned back on the couch, bracing herself against the soft cushions. She could easily imagine how his mother had felt, how she herself would
feel faced with the prospect of Amanda moving hundreds of miles away.

"She wanted to come here, to the University of
Wisconsin. I visited the campus with her once. Good
school. Nice town. Low crime rate. So I encouraged
her to go, despite Mama's objections. I paid for her
tuition, her dorm and her bus ticket."

The rumble of his voice stopped, leaving nothing
but the labored sound of his breathing. His eyes
seemed to grow blacker, void of light.

The clock ticked out the seconds from the corner
of the room. A minute passed. He drew in a deep
breath. "A month later, Janey's body was found naked in a muddy ditch."

Against her will, Jacqueline gasped out loud. She
shook her head, trying to banish the horrible picture
from her mind, his aching grief echoing in her ears.

He shook his head slowly. "I quit my job and took
a job with the district attorney's office up here. I
wanted to be near the investigation, to keep an eye
on things, I guess. But it didn't do any good. We

never found the snake who killed Janey. She can never have justice. But Mark can. And Val can.''

She looked down at the picture in her trembling hand. It was so clear to her now. His obsession. His drive. His commitment to winning justice for murder victims. ''This is all for your sister. Your crusade. Your obsession with justice. All to make up for the justice that she'll never have.''

''And it will never be enough.'' He lifted his eyes and he looked down at her, those sharp black eyes boring past her defenses. ''No matter what I do, it will never be enough.''

She closed her eyes, shutting out his pain, his crippling guilt. She didn't want to know this much about Dillon Reese. She wanted to hold on to her anger toward him, to wrap it around her like a protective cloak. She wanted to blame him for Mark's death, for the danger Amanda faced. She didn't want to feel for him, ache for him, understand his drive more clearly than she understood her own heart.

She leaned forward, elbows on knees, and cradled her head in her hands. When she'd first met Dillon she'd believed there could be something between them, something special. God knew there was plenty of sexual attraction sizzling in the air when they were together. She had only to remember the night she'd received the first threatening phone call from Swain, the night Dillon had held her in his arms. The warmth of his body wrapping around her, the hard strength of his chest as she'd laid her cheek against him, the electric charge that had raced along her nerves, making her feel more alive than ever before.

But it was more than that, more than just sexual.

They seemed to share an understanding, a bond. She'd even entertained fantasies of asking him to dinner some evening after her impending divorce from Mark was finalized and after she had gotten back on her feet.

But that had all changed when the threats started. She'd seen then how vulnerable Amanda and she were. She'd seen then that Mark cared more about being a celebrity than about his daughter. She'd seen then that Dillon was more driven by his need for justice than by a desire to do what was right for Amanda or for her. The fantasy had crumbled.

After that, she'd built walls, brick by brick, to protect Amanda and herself from the mess Mark had made of their old life. And she'd built walls around her heart to protect herself from trusting a man again—especially Dillon Reese.

And now Dillon's pain had scaled those walls. But she couldn't let him swing a leg over the top. Dillon was about justice, pure and simple. And now that she understood the reason behind his crusade, she could see how misguided her long-ago fantasies of him were. Because Dillon had no room in his heart for anything but justice. And she'd suffered too much heartbreak to take a chance on something that could never be.

He leaned toward her. ''Are you all right?''

Jacqueline nodded but didn't look up at him.

''Now you understand why I will go to any lengths to keep your daughter safe.''

Yes, she did understand. Amanda was the key to locking Swain away, to winning justice for Mark and Val, to helping Dillon pay his debt to his sister. He'd sacrifice everything to protect her little girl, of this she now had no doubt. She only prayed it would be enough.

"I DON'T KILL CHILDREN." Buck Swain ground out the stub of his cigarette in the overflowing ashtray and scowled into the telephone. How in hell was he supposed to explain a thing like honor to someone who had none?

"Unless you want to add to Reese's conviction record, you'd damn well better start."

"If you want the girl dead so bad, kill her yourself."

"She didn't see me."

"But if I go down, you go down. Remember that."

"I've had it with your blackmail, Swain. If it wasn't for your incompetence, this whole mess would be behind us."

The familiar pressure started to build in Swain's head, rattling in his ears like the discharge of an M-16. He gripped the phone tight in his bad hand until it creaked with the pressure. Despite the missing fingers, despite the scorched skin and damaged nerves, he still had enough strength in the hand to break the cheap plastic. Or crush a human trachea. The person on the other end of the line would be wise to take that into account. "Go to hell."

"I should just let Reese have at you."

Contempt twisted Swain's gut. Dillon Reese. The lying SOB. Even the name made his blood heat, his trigger finger ache. He'd had to sit in that damned courtroom day after day and listen to Reese's lies.

Lies maligning Swain's honor, his dignity. As if Reese had any idea what true honor was. He hadn't served his country. He hadn't laid his life on the line as Swain had. How dare Reese or any of them judge what they didn't understand? "How am I supposed to off the girl if I don't know where she is? You said Reese didn't tell anyone in the task force where he was taking the girl and her mother."

"I'll find out where he's hiding them. Leave that part to me. You be ready to take care of the girl. And her mother, just to be safe."

The mother. It didn't take much effort to remember the mother. Jacqueline Schettler had the kind of body a man didn't forget easily. But good-looking or not, Swain wouldn't have any trouble taking her out. Without a second thought he'd squeezed off the round that had killed the blond bartender. He had slit Liz's throat as easily as gutting a deer. Killing adult women didn't bother him. As long as he had a reason.

But killing a child...

Damn the people who'd forced him into this mess. Liz with her open thighs and loose lips. Mark Schettler, the nosy, fame-seeking bastard who'd witnessed him disposing of his bloody clothes after Liz's murder. Jacqueline Schettler for going to the cops after he'd warned her to get out of state. Dillon Reese, the self-righteous attack dog, for standing up in a packed courtroom and spouting lie after lie. Damn them all. He pulled a battered pack of cigarettes from his pocket and shook one free. God, he needed a smoke.

"Well, Swain?"

Tapping the cigarette's filter on the scarred table

in front of him, Swain scowled into the phone once again. Good thing he wasn't meeting this two-faced fraud in person. The hypocrite would probably want to shake hands on the deal. Maybe Swain would offer his bad hand with the slick, burned skin and the missing fingers, just to watch the disgust creep over that pious, holier-than-thou face. "Fine. I'll take out the girl. It's a deal, *partner*."

Swain could almost feel the revulsion reaching out over the phone line. Smiling, he slipped the cigarette between his lips.

Chapter Six

Dillon leaned his elbows on the desktop and stared into the darkened hall leading to the bedroom. Jacqueline had gone to bed over an hour ago, and he'd been staring ever since. Staring and thinking.

Jacqueline's questions echoed in his mind. She'd picked up on his desperation, his driving need for justice, and now she knew how deep his need ran.

Automatically his fingers pulled his wallet from his pocket and flipped open the leather flap. Slipping out the battered picture, he cradled it gently in his hands.

Janey. His little sister Janey. So young and fresh. So eager to take on the world. So full of the joy of life. Pain twisted in his chest like the thrust of a dull and rusty blade.

He'd never told anyone about Janey, about his need to avenge her death, about his need to absolve his own guilt. It was too raw, too personal to explain. But he'd told the story to Jacqueline. He'd torn open his private hell and laid it at her feet.

And she'd listened. She'd looked into the emptiness yawning inside him like a gully long since dry, and she'd understood. He'd seen it in her eyes.

A longing assaulted him. Longing so open and raw it took his breath away. How he yearned to know Jacqueline better. How he yearned to do normal things like take her to dinner and hold her in his arms and talk to her about the future. How he yearned to be more to her than a bodyguard and she more to him than a witness.

But all the yearning in the world couldn't change anything.

Tucking the photo back in its place, he reached for the key stashed under the top of his desk, unlocked the top drawer and slid it open. Cloaked in shadow, his .357 Colt Defender lay in the bottom of the drawer. Cleaned, loaded and ready. He lifted the revolver, its weight reassuring in his hand, the dim glow of the nearly full moon reflecting off its nickel-plated finish.

He might not be able to be everything he wanted to Jacqueline, but he could keep her and her daughter safe until he was able to put Swain away.

And once that happened, they could go back to their lives. And he would go on to the next case. And the next. Until he finally joined his family in that little burial plot outside Amarillo. Only then would it be over. Only then could he rest.

A SCREAM SHREDDED the night. Dillon jolted awake. The bedroom. Jacqueline. Heart hammering, he reached under the couch. His fingers brushed cold, hard metal.

The scream pierced the air again.

Grasping the Defender, he sprang to his feet and raced through the dark maze of the living room and into the blackness of the narrow hall.

He reached for the bedroom doorknob, shoved the door open and readied his weapon.

Shadowed figures tangled together on the bed. Jacqueline and her daughter? An intruder? The shuttered window blinds blocked the moon's glow. Damn this unrelenting darkness. He couldn't see a thing. Heart pounding, he flicked on the light.

Jacqueline spun around, staring up at him, eyes wide, skin pale. Seeing the gun, she shielded Amanda with her body. "It's okay. It's okay. Amanda had a nightmare."

Dillon swept the room with his gaze. No Swain. No high-powered rifle or razor-sharp knife. Only a little girl's nightmare. He lifted the gun, pointing the barrel at the ceiling. Scooping breath after breath into his lungs, he tried to slow the adrenaline pounding through him. He settled his gaze on Jacqueline.

Wearing one of his old T-shirts, she huddled on the bed, even more thin and delicate than she had looked in her baggy clothing. The shirt had ridden up in her awkward pose, showing a wisp of white lace panties. Her long bare legs curled on top of the navy sheets and comforter, her skin creamy against the dark linens.

His mouth went dry.

He knew he should look away, not take advantage of her shock, her fear, not leer at her like a teenage boy seeing his first glimpse of a woman's underwear. But he couldn't tear his eyes from her.

Jacqueline lifted her gaze from the revolver in his

hand and met his eyes. "She's all right. We're all right," she whispered.

He dragged his eyes from her and tucked the gun into his waistband, the metal pressing against the small of his back.

Soft mewing came from the bed behind Jacqueline, each sound so heartbreaking, Dillon nearly flinched. Amanda. The poor kid. How could anyone know the horror of what that little girl was going through? He circled the bed.

She sat propped against the pillow, strands of chestnut hair stuck to her wet cheeks. Her teary eyes focused on him.

His heart twisted in his chest. She looked so much like Janey had at the same age. Janey's big blue eyes had glistened in the same way when she was afraid. When she needed her big brother to comfort her.

He'd loved playing Janey's knight in shining armor when she'd awakened with nightmares. Loved sitting in her dark room, her little bubble-bath-scented body cuddled into the crook of his arm, her eyes raised to him in adoration. Quite the power trip for an awkward teenage boy. But that was a long time ago. Back when he thought he could save her from the horrors of the world.

He pulled himself from his memories and focused on the little girl in front of him now. "When my baby sister woke up with nightmares, I used to tell her a story. It made her feel better."

Amanda choked back a sob and studied him as though she couldn't imagine him having a family. Her fingers latched on to a shank of her chestnut hair, twisting it into a tight rope.

"I'd tell her the story of a filly on our ranch that grew up to be a champion. Do you want to hear that story?"

Amanda's nod was so slight, Dillon couldn't be sure if he'd witnessed it at all. "If it's all right with your mama, I'll tell you the story I used to tell Janey."

Jacqueline pulled her gaze from her daughter and scanned Dillon's face. Her expression was soft with compassion. Drawing in a shaky breath, she leaned down and kissed her daughter on the cheek. "Roll over on your tummy, punkin, and listen to Mr. Reese's story. Everything is going to be okay."

Amanda looked from her mother to Dillon, fear shadowing her eyes and puckering her little mouth. After sizing up the situation, she rolled onto her stomach. Head turned to face Dillon, she looked up at him with those expectant blue eyes, as if waiting for him to sweep her fears away.

Jacqueline moved her hand over her daughter's back, love evident with each rhythmic stroke. But her eyes remained glued to him. Her unspoken message was plain as a boil on a pug nose. *I'm trusting you with my daughter's fragile emotions. Don't blow it.*

Dillon cleared his throat and drew a fortifying breath. "I grew up on a ranch. From the time I can remember, my daddy raised Black Angus cattle and some pretty decent cutting horses. But way back when I was a boy, a filly was born that was special. The moment she took her first wobbly step, my daddy promised me that she would be my first real cutting horse."

Amanda's cheeks seemed to relax, and her mouth

lost its frightened pucker. The story was working its magic, just as it had on Janey.

"But there was one problem. She was skittish as the day is long. Everything scared her. The lighting of a bird on a fence post, the clanging of a grain bucket at dinnertime, every sound or movement."

Worry crinkled Amanda's brow.

He offered her a reassuring smile. "The filly grew up into a strapping young horse, and when she turned two, my daddy threw a saddle on her back for the first time. It took a long time and a lot of patience, but finally he broke her to ride. The next step was to show her the cattle. When she saw her first Black Angus, she nearly bolted from the pen. She wouldn't go near the cattle. My daddy tried for months to get her to approach them, but she wouldn't. She was too frightened. So one day my daddy told me he was turning her out with the broodmares. She'd never be a cutting horse. He'd find me another horse to show."

Amanda frowned, her face so sad it pulled on Dillon's heart. In the face of the filly's plight, she'd forgotten all about the nightmare her life had become.

"So my daddy did what he said and turned his attention to some of the other young stock. And one day a big Black Angus bull in the next pasture noticed the grass in the broodmares' pasture looked greener and more delicious. So he broke down the fence separating the pastures. Well, the grass was delicious. So delicious, in fact, that he decided he wanted it all to himself. He started chasing the mares. The horses ran away from him easily at first. But after a few hours, they started to get tired. Then the filly's mother stepped in a gopher hole and hurt her foot. She couldn't run away from the bull anymore.''

Amanda drew in a sharp breath. A whimper sounded from deep in her throat. Though Jacqueline still ran her hand soothingly over her daughter's hair, her eyes narrowed to warning slits.

He hurried to the end of his story. ''The bull was mad by this time. Really mad. He decided to take out his anger on the filly's mother. He lowered his sharp horns and charged her. And who stepped in front of the injured mare but the frightened filly herself. She lowered her head and charged the bull right back. The sight of the filly charging scared the bull so much, he stopped in his tracks, spun around and ran away. Using cutting talent that we always knew she had, the filly chased the bull back into his own pasture and stood guard until my daddy fixed the break in the fence. And the filly was never afraid of cattle again.''

''And the mommy horse was okay?'' Amanda's little brow creased with worry.

''Yes. Her foot healed up and she was fine. And she was very proud of her daughter for being so brave and facing the bull.''

A trembling smile struggled to appear on Amanda's lips. ''I'm brave like that.''

Dillon's throat closed. ''I know you're brave, darlin'. Very brave.''

Jacqueline leaned down and kissed Amanda on the cheek, her long chestnut hair falling like a curtain around her daughter's face. Turning from her daughter, she looked up at Dillon. Her chin trembled. Her eyes filled with tears. "Thank you."

The tremor in her voice knocked the breath out of him. He didn't move. He didn't breathe. All he could do was stare at this beautiful, vulnerable woman and her sweet little girl.

Growing up, he'd always assumed that one day he would have a wife and children. He'd have this sweetness, this intimacy as a part of his daily life. But after Janey's death, things had changed. He had changed. And a family was no longer an option.

But it wasn't until now that he'd really been able to feel what he'd given up.

JACQUELINE'S EYES OPENED as the first rays of dawn filtered through the miniblinds covering the windows of Dillon's bedroom. Beside her, Amanda's breathing was soft and steady. Visions of the night before crowded into her mind. Amanda's scream, Dillon appearing at the door with that hideous-looking gun, his horse story and its soothing effect on her little girl. He had made quite an impression on her daughter with his tale. Jacqueline couldn't forget the determination shining in Amanda's eyes by the end of his story. And she was more than grateful for Amanda's peaceful sleep that followed. Sleep for which she had Dillon Reese to thank.

If only Jacqueline could have slept. Every bone in her body ached. Every cell in her brain throbbed. She'd give almost anything to be able to slip into a deep sleep, free from worry, free from fear, free from the helplessness that nearly suffocated her. But she could never attain such peace. Not until Amanda was safe.

Careful not to disturb her daughter, she hoisted her body from the bed. All she needed was a hot shower and a cup of black coffee. Then she would be stronger. Then she could face another day.

She pulled on her jeans, opened the door and padded across the cool hardwood floor to the bathroom, her bare feet making no noise.

As if in a daze, she turned on the shower and faced the mirror. Dark shadows lurked under her eyes. The pallor of her skin nearly matched the white T-shirt she wore.

A T-shirt. That's all she'd been wearing when Dillon had burst into the room last night. She pressed her hands to her cheeks, her skin hot to the touch. Why hadn't she covered herself? Why had she frozen, staring at him as if he'd pulled the gun on her?

She knew why.

She had wanted his gaze to travel over her bare legs. She'd relished the desire in his eyes. She'd soaked it in the way the frozen earth soaked in the first warm rays of spring. And she'd wanted more. Even now she wanted more.

She turned away from the mirror. She had to get her thoughts under control. Nothing was going to happen between Dillon and her. Nothing could. She had a daughter to protect and raise. And Dillon.... Dillon had a crusade to fight.

A hot shower, followed by a steaming cup of coffee, that's what she needed to get her life and her errant feelings in perspective. Hurriedly she stripped off her clothes and climbed into the shower. Hot water and thick, fragrant shampoo washed over her hair and sluiced down her body. Finally when her skin had started to prune she flicked off the water and grabbed for a towel.

She dried herself and pulled on her sweater and jeans. What she wouldn't give for a change of clothes. But her suitcase, along with Amanda's, was still in the back seat of her car, probably locked in some police garage. She would have to ask Dillon if they could get it back.

Dillon. At the thought of him, her pulse picked up its pace and a shiver traveled over her skin. She rubbed her hands over her arms and turned off her mind.

Coffee. She'd follow through with the second part of her morning's plan. She'd make coffee and breakfast—a breakfast to thank Dillon for his story last night, for Amanda's night of peaceful sleep. And most of all, she'd pray that she could keep her mind from wandering off in directions better left unexplored.

DILLON HUNG UP THE PHONE and hefted himself out of his desk chair. The scent of frying eggs, browning toast and brewing coffee tantalized his nostrils and made his mouth water. The delectable smells had teased him the entire time he'd been on the phone with Mylinski planning their next move.

If he was going to catch Swain and his informant, he needed access to certain files in the D.A.'s office. And he couldn't risk having them delivered to his house. Which meant he had to leave the house, leave Jacqueline and Amanda, and go get them.

But first, breakfast. He eased his way into the kitchen.

Jacqueline stood at the old gas stove, steam rising from two frying pans in front of her. Even dressed in the wrinkled, shapeless jeans and sweater from yesterday, she looked sexy as hell. Almost as sexy as she had last night with her long bare legs tangled in his sheets.

He pulled his gaze from her and focused on Amanda, who sat at the kitchen table swinging her dangling little legs in a crazy rhythm.

An uneasy feeling pricked the back of his neck. It had been a long time since he'd shared breakfast with anyone. Longer still since someone had actually cooked for him. And he wasn't sure it was a good idea. Not sure at all.

Jacqueline and her daughter had already worked their way under his skin like a pair of damned chiggers. He didn't need to get any more involved with them. But he couldn't seem to stop himself. And a cozy Saturday-morning breakfast wasn't about to make it any easier.

He grabbed two coffee cups from the cupboard. Sneaking the pot out from under the automatic drip coffeemaker, he filled both cups and set one on the counter near Jacqueline.

She turned to him with a quiet smile. "Thank you."

For a moment he just stared at her. Never before had he seen such a beautiful smile. Her eyes, wide and blue as a Texas sky, crinkled slightly at the corners. Her square, drill-sergeant jaw softened. And the cutest dimple he'd ever seen dented one smooth cheek.

"No problem. I was pouring myself a cup anyway." He brought the scalding-hot coffee to his lips and gulped.

"Not just for the coffee. For telling me the truth about your sister. For being there for Amanda last night."

She sounded grateful. And behind the words he sensed a loneliness, a vulnerability that turned the warning prickle at the back of his neck into a full-fledged ache. "Just doing my job."

She drew herself up, her grin fading, her dimple disappearing in her smooth cheek. "Well, job or not, you went the extra mile. I really do appreciate all you've done for us."

What could he say? You're welcome? Just part of the job, ma'am? Glad to do it? Any response he could come up with seemed too shallow, almost flip. He'd already made her withdraw. He didn't want to do even more damage. The reality was that if he hadn't encouraged Mark to testify, Amanda wouldn't be needing his comfort now.

Jacqueline seemed to accept his silence, and turned back to her breakfast preparation. Using the spatula, she rolled the omelettes out of the pans and onto plates. She handed him two of the plates, and they sat at the table next to Amanda.

Dillon took another gulp of scalding coffee and shoveled a forkful of eggs into his mouth. The tangy cheddar and the fluffy, buttery eggs melted on his tongue. "Delicious."

She nodded. "Thank you. Glad you like them."

"I do."

For a moment her eyes lingered on him, as if she expected him to say more. Then she turned her attention back to the eggs in front of her. Across the table Amanda picked at her food and watched him speculatively.

Silence stretched between them like a chasm waiting to be bridged. He shifted in his chair. He stuffed another bite of eggs into his mouth and chewed. He'd never been one to be uncomfortable with silence. In fact, he'd used it as a tool more than once. It was surprising how many defendants were more concerned with filling an awkward silence than with hiding their sins.

Even more surprising was that right this moment he understood what they must have felt. He searched his mind for something benign to say. He'd never been good at small talk, but it was worth a shot. "How did you get into the brew pub business?"

Her brow furrowed at his awkward attempt. "My dad opened the brew pub when I was a kid. He used to let me go to work with him on Saturday mornings. I'd chew on malted barley and watch him work."

As her melodic voice, deep and rich as the dark roast coffee, resonated through the room, the muscles in Dillon's shoulders relaxed a little.

Still eyeing him curiously, Jacqueline sipped her coffee and nodded. "My dad loved making beer. He'd spend hour after hour experimenting with different malts, yeasts, hops. You should have seen the excitement on his face when he worked." A slight smile played over her lips at remembering.

"It must have been contagious."

"Must have been. The only thing I ever wanted to do was work with my dad in the pub. I studied in Germany to be a brewmaster. Then I worked in a microbrewery in Oregon for a couple of years. But I always wanted to come back here and work alongside my dad in the pub he started. And I finally did. I guess I was a chip off the old block."

Her smile turned wistful, then sad. "When he died, my mother moved back to Germany and I took over the pub on my own. It was called Der Brauhaus back then. We changed the name to Schettler Brew Pub when I married Mark."

"It's been quite a success, I understand. It seems packed every night."

"My dad wasn't much of a businessman and neither am I. Mark made the place the financial success it is." She paused for a moment, her eyes sparking with enthusiasm. "But the beer, that was my domain. The beer has won just about every major award in North America. Three years ago, my Doppelbock won a gold medal at the Great American Beer Festival."

"You must be very proud."

She shrugged. "The prizes and money were great, don't get me wrong, but the best part was the day-to-day operation. Trying new blends of malts, hops and yeasts. Experimenting. Creating."

He couldn't help picking up a tone of sadness in her voice, a note of regret. "If you owned the pub before you married, why did you give it up?"

"Mark wanted it." She glanced at her daughter, who was quietly eating her omelette. "I did what I had to."

Dillon gritted his teeth. Obviously Mark had traded the brew pub for custody of Amanda. What kind of man would force his wife to make a choice like that? And what kind of a man would use his daughter as a bargaining chip?

He'd known even before the night Jacqueline had received the first threatening phone call and Mark had refused to come home from his party to protect and comfort her that her husband was a self-centered worm. This new revelation didn't come as a surprise. Neither did the anger boiling inside him. "He was wrong to force you to make that choice. He shouldn't have gotten away with it."

Returning her gaze to him, she gave a casual shrug of her shoulders as if losing her beloved brew pub mattered about as much as a hangnail. But try as she might, she couldn't mask the regret in her eyes. "I took a job as a secretary with a local construction company. It was a good job."

"But it wasn't the work you loved," he finished. She was amazing. In an age when many parents weren't even willing to give up a little of their time for their children, Jacqueline had given up everything—her career, her home, her life. He thought of the way she'd vacated her house yesterday morning on her way out of state. Seemingly nothing had been disturbed, nothing was out of the ordinary except the empty table that had once been covered with family photos. She'd taken nothing with her but a few changes of clothes, the pictures and her memories. Once again she'd left her life behind to save her daughter.

And this time it was him and his fight for justice that had caused it.

He massaged the back of his throbbing neck and dropped his gaze to the plate in front of him. He needed some air. And more than that, he needed some time away from Jacqueline. Because the time when he'd been able to keep objective about this case was long past. And his feelings for her were getting more personal with each moment he spent breathing in her vanilla scent.

Jacqueline watched Dillon look down at the eggs and cheddar congealing on his plate as if he didn't have any idea what they were or how they got there. He pushed the plate back and stood. "Detective Mylinski has some files I need to pick up. I'm going to have to leave for a little while."

"Leave?" Her heart stuttered. She shot from her chair, standing on shaky legs. "You can't."

Amanda looked up from her plate, her eyes widening.

Jacqueline took a calming breath and offered her daughter a little smile. "It's okay, punkin. Mr. Reese just surprised me."

When Amanda turned back to her food, Jacqueline moved closer to Dillon and lowered her voice. "You can't leave. What if—" She broke off, hoping Dillon would get the gist without her putting those frightful words out where Amanda could hear them.

"No one knows you're here. You're safe. And if I'm going to figure out who is behind the leak in the task force, I need those files. I won't be gone long."

Hollowness descended into the pit of her stomach.

Long or not, she and Amanda would be alone in this house in the middle of the woods. At one time being free of Dillon was all she wanted. Now the thought filled her with dread.

"I'll leave my gun with you."

The gun. Jacqueline's mind recoiled at the thought. She'd never held a gun in her life. Until Dillon had burst into the bedroom in reaction to Amanda's scream last night, she'd never even seen one except on television or in the movies. She didn't want to see or touch one now. And she definitely didn't want one of the hideous things near her child.

She glanced at Amanda. Her little girl stabbed her fork into the omelette on her plate and twirled, cheddar twisting around the tines like storm clouds around a hurricane's eye.

As much as Jacqueline abhorred guns, she would do what she must to protect her daughter. And if arming herself was the only way, she'd strap on a whole arsenal. "I've never shot a gun before."

Dillon's eyebrows pulled together in a frown. He lowered his voice to a rough whisper. "Could you pull the trigger? If he was coming at you, could you use it?"

She didn't have to glance in Amanda's direction this time. She raised her chin. "I'll do whatever I have to."

"You can't hesitate. Even for a second. If you do, he could take it away from you. It would be worse than not having a weapon at all."

She swallowed and drew a deep breath, trying to quiet her jangling nerves. "If you teach me how to use it, I'll use it. I won't let him hurt my little girl."

Though barely above a whisper, her voice sounded strong and sure and determined, even to her own ears.

He leveled his black gaze on her and nodded. "Maybe there's something on television Amanda would like to watch. I'll be waiting in the living room."

It didn't take long to settle Amanda in front of the Batman cartoon, and soon Jacqueline was standing in the living room, reaching trembling fingers toward the gun in Dillon's hand.

"Don't worry. It won't go off. I unloaded it." He flipped open the cylinder to show her. "See? It's perfectly safe."

A bubble of laughter caught in her throat. Hysterical laughter. Panicky laughter. The gun looked perfectly safe. It looked like a shiny new toy. A Lone Ranger cap gun that belonged holstered around a little boy's waist.

Bang, bang, you're dead.

She shuddered as her fingers touched its cold nickel-plated finish. This gun was no toy. It was hideously real. "Bullets or no, this thing isn't perfectly safe. Not in my hands, anyway."

His low chuckle was warm, reassuring. He moved behind her, his chest brushing her back, his arms circling her in an embrace.

She soaked in the warmth of his arms, of his body, and struggled to keep her mind on the gun.

He pressed it into her fist. Covering her hand with his, he molded her palm and fingers around the weapon's handle. His hands were big and engulfed hers, his skin deliciously rough. "I'll let you get the feel for it before I show you how to load it."

The gun's leaden weight settled in her hand, straining the muscles in her wrist and arm. She gritted her teeth and tried to hold it steady, but despite her effort, the barrel dipped and bobbed. "It's heavy. I can hardly lift it."

"You'll need to use two hands." Dillon found her other hand and positioned it on the gun. "It also helps if you lean against something like a doorjamb or piece of furniture to steady yourself. Here. Lean back against me."

She braced herself and leaned back against his broad chest. His warmth seeped into her. His scent swirled through her.

He snuggled up behind her, fitting his body intimately with hers. "Stand with your feet about shoulder-width apart. This foot slightly back from the other." He brushed the outside of her thigh.

A wave of heat spread through her. She bit her bottom lip. Concentrating on the weapon in her hands, she stretched the gun out in front of her and adopted a pose she remembered Angie Dickinson using in the opening of the old television show *Police Woman*.

"Good, but keep your left elbow slightly bent or the gun's recoil will make you unsteady." He pressed the inside of her elbow with his fingertips, guiding her to the proper position.

She eyed the barrel of the gun, unmoving now in her outstretched arms. "How do I aim it?"

"If Swain is coming after you, you won't have time to aim. Just point at the center of his body and shoot. You've got to make every second count. Pretend the door is him.''

She did as he instructed, pointing at the middle of the front door. She closed her eyes, tensed her shoulders and jerked back on the trigger. A dull click came from the weapon.

''Let's try that again,'' he said patiently, his breath tickling her cheek. ''This time keep your eyes open.''

She hadn't even realized she'd closed her eyes. If Swain had been coming at her, it would be all over. ''Right. Eyes open.''

''And try not to tense up.'' His warm hands cupped the muscles of her shoulders, gently massaging. ''Tensed shoulders make for poor shots. Take a deep breath and let it out while lowering your shoulders. At the end of the exhale, that's when you fire.''

''Got it.'' She stretched the gun out in front of her.

''Instead of pulling the trigger, think about squeezing it. Slowly.''

His voice, so gentle and close to her ear, conjured up images of hands roaming over bare skin...slowly squeezing. She drew in a shaky breath.

''Now exhale and lower your shoulders.''

She let the air stream from pursed lips and lowered her shoulders.

''Now squeeze.'' His smoky drawl washed over her, and with it both chills and fire.

She squeezed the trigger. The gun clicked.

She could feel him smile. ''That's my girl.''

She let his praise wrap around her, soak into her like the heat of his body.

''So, do you feel safer?''

His question caught her off guard. Now that she

could fire a gun, now that she could defend herself and her daughter, did she feel safer?

No.

But it wasn't the hunk of metal in her fists she had to blame. It was something far more dangerous. The heat of his body, snug against her, the whisper of his breath in her ear.

It didn't make sense. He was a man with a personal crusade, a man who lived and breathed justice, a man who, as soon as this case was over, would go on to the next and leave her and Amanda far behind.

But his touch tempted her to forget all these things. Each sensation was loaded. And the feelings smoldering within her were far from safe.

Chapter Seven

Dillon flipped the truck's sun visor down, adjusted his sunglasses to fight the sun's glare off the rows of cars in the mall parking lot and leaned back in the seat to wait. And think.

Damn. This morning's breakfast with Jacqueline had shaken him down to the leather soles of his Tony Lama boots. He didn't even have to close his eyes to picture the passion she had for her former life as a brewmaster. Her squint-eyed determination when learning to fire his gun.

And he would never forget the feel of her body against him. Her softness, her scent. It was scorched into his mind like a brand on a calf's hide.

He pinched the bridge of his nose between thumb and forefinger. He had to get his mind *off* Jacqueline and *on* his case against Swain. It was the only way he could help her, the only way he could ensure her daughter's safety. He needed justice in this case. Not just for himself, not just for Swain's victims, but so Jacqueline could take her little girl and return to the life she'd been forced to give up—that *he'd* forced her to give up. To the happiness she deserved.

And *that* was what had brought him to the bustling parking lot of West Towne Mall. The files.

He checked his watch. Two o'clock. Time to move. He dismounted from the truck. After slipping his key into a magnetic key box, he fastened it under the truck's trailer hitch and set out across the parking lot.

He bypassed the mall's entrance, striding around the building's periphery instead. His boot heels thunked on the pavement. It felt good to stretch his legs, to draw the frosty air deep into his lungs. At least he was doing something. Taking a step toward finding the snake who had fed Mark's and Valerie's whereabouts to Swain.

It didn't take long for him to reach the opposite side of the mall. He scanned the parking lot. Sandwiched between a minivan and a sports-utility vehicle, Al Mylinski's ancient blue Impala caught his eye. Good old Mylinski. Right on time as usual.

He examined the lot again, this time looking for anyone watching the car. A woman herded her flock of children toward the mall's entrance. A couple marched toward their car, engrossed in an animated argument. No sign of Swain. Mylinski had either lost him in traffic, or Swain had followed the detective into the mall on his shopping excursion.

Dillon strode across the parking lot. Reaching the Impala, he ran a hand under the car's front bumper. His fingers hit a small metal box like the one he'd attached to his truck's bumper. He detached the box and removed the Impala's keys, unlocked the door and folded himself behind the wheel. He glanced into the back seat. Two boxes of files perched on the worn vinyl upholstery. Personnel files. Case files. Two paisley-print suitcases peeked out from behind the boxes. And three bags of groceries sat on the floor.

Everything he needed.

He slipped the key into the ignition. The car sputtered, then roared to life. He shifted the car into gear and headed back to Jacqueline, Amanda and some answers.

"WHERE THE HELL WERE YOU?" the voice blared from the phone receiver.

Buck Swain clenched the phone in his bad hand until the slick red knuckles turned pale. He wasn't about to tell anyone that he'd spent the morning traipsing through a shopping mall. That he'd been so intent on shadowing the bald detective that he hadn't realized, until Mylinski climbed into Reese's pickup, that he'd been had. "What do you want?"

"I want you to stay by the damned phone like we agreed."

Swain ground out his cigarette butt in the overflowing ashtray. "Agreed, my ass," he mumbled under his breath. He hadn't agreed to anything. He'd been ordered. "Get to the point. Why're you calling?"

"I think I know where the girl is."

A jolt of adrenaline shot through Swain's bloodstream. "Where?"

"I have one last thing to check out. I'll know if my hunch is right by tonight."

Tonight. He reached into his shirt pocket and pulled out a pack of cigarettes. Plucking one from the pack, he tapped the filter on the table before lighting up. He didn't like killing kids, but he'd get over it. It was a choice between him and her, after all. And he *wasn't* going to spend even one day in prison.

He took a deep drag, filling his lungs with smoke. Hate ate at his gut. Hate for the coward on the other end of the line. A coward who had no problem barking orders from justice's ivory tower, but would never—could never—pull the trigger or drag a knife across an outstretched throat and feel the shudder as life left a human body.

No. Murder was too distasteful, too messy for a weasel like this. "Bullet or knife?" he goaded.

The voice on the other end of the phone hesitated. "Just do it. I don't want to know how."

He could imagine the shudder. He prodded further. "And the mother? How do you want her done?"

Again the voice hesitated.

Damn coward.

"Do whatever you have to do, Swain. I'll call tonight. Stay by the phone until I do."

Swain sneered into the receiver. Do whatever he had to. Exactly what he'd intended to do from the first—what he had to. No matter who got in the way.

PERCHED ON THE EDGE of the bed, Jacqueline moved her hand over Amanda's back in time to the soft sigh of her little girl's breathing. Afternoon sunlight slanted through the shuttered blind on the window, casting a pattern of yellow lines on the navy comforter. For the fifth time in five minutes she eyed the glowing numbers of the alarm clock sitting on the tall chest of drawers. Ten minutes to two.

Dillon hadn't been gone long, she told herself. But her stomach tightened anyway. The hour since he'd left Amanda and her alone in the house seemed like forever.

She dragged her gaze from the clock, pausing on the gun resting next to it. The muted sunlight reflected off the polished silver barrel.

Shuddering, she looked away from the obscene thing and back at her sleeping daughter. Her arms ached to hold Amanda, to press that precious little body to her breast and never let go. Not until this nightmare was over. She brushed her lips on Amanda's forehead. Inhaling deeply, she drew her little girl's scent into her soul. Warm sleep and peanut butter.

Tears blurred Jacqueline's vision.

She'd wanted her daughter to grow up the way she had. She'd wanted her to have a safe childhood. An innocent childhood.

Not a childhood full of danger. Not innocence marred by murder and guns.

A sob she couldn't contain racked her body. She pressed her hand over her mouth, stifling the sound. The last thing she wanted to do was wake Amanda.

She stood, forced her feet to carry her to the chest of drawers and lifted the gun gingerly by the grip. Slipping out of the room, she left the door open a crack and flicked on the hall light. A shaft of light shone into the room, a beacon if Amanda should wake after darkness fell. After one last glance through a haze of tears at her peacefully sleeping daughter, she made her way down the short hall toward the living room. Once there, she lowered herself into the soft embrace of the couch.

She set the gun on the cushion next to her and allowed tears to flow silently down her cheeks and drip off her chin. Tears for Mark, for Val, for herself, but mostly for Amanda. For the childhood she'd lost. For the innocence she'd never have again.

Her eyes burned, her lower lids felt as swollen as if a fist had pummeled them and her body ached with exhaustion. But she couldn't stop crying.

Not until the rattle of a car entering the driveway cut the silent room like a hail of gunfire.

The sound wasn't the low growl of Dillon's truck but the high-pitched wheeze of a car on its last legs. Dashing the tears from her eyes with the back of her hand, she grabbed the gun from the cushion beside her and ran to the kitchen window. Parting the blinds ever so slightly, she peered out at the driveway.

A rust-pocked blue car pulled into the detached garage. A car she'd never seen before. A stranger's car.

Her blood turned to ice. She fitted the gun into her hands and rested a trembling finger on the trigger, the grip slippery in her sweaty palm. Holding her breath, she waited for the driver to emerge from the vehicle and approach the house.

The car door opened.

Dillon stepped out.

Her knees swayed. Relief pounded through her head. Slumping against the window frame, she lowered the barrel, pointing it to the floor in front of her.

Letting the gun dangle in one hand, she ran her

fingers through her tangled hair and wiped her tears-tained cheeks dry with the other. She didn't want him to know she'd been crying. Somehow her momentary breakdown was too intimate, too personal to share with anyone.

When Dillon finally walked in the kitchen door, a large cardboard box in his arms, her breathing had slowed somewhat. His black eyes took in her face and the gun in her shaking hand. Concern widened his eyes. He set the box on a kitchen chair and stepped toward her, so close she could feel his body heat emanating from him in waves. "What happened?"

She met his eyes. Dragging in a deep breath, she tried to inject levity into her voice. "Nice car. New? I hope you didn't pay too much for it."

His brow pinched with concern. "Oh God, I didn't think. The last thing I wanted to do was scare you. I'm sorry. I traded vehicles with Detective Mylinski."

She offered him a shaky smile. It wasn't much as smiles go, but it was the best she could manage.

He reached toward her, removed the gun from her fingers and tucked it into the waistband of his jeans. "Those tears didn't come from my driving a strange car into the driveway. Are you going to tell me what's wrong?"

She forced her best imitation of a casual shrug. "Just catching up, I guess."

The harsh lines of his face became drawn with guilt. "I'm sorry."

His tone was so sincere, so tender, she wanted to curl up in the smoky rumble of it. She gnawed on her lower lip and opened her eyes wide to keep the tears from escaping. "I'll be all right. I was just—" Her voice gave way. A tear caught in her lashes before it trickled a hot trail down one cheek. She dashed it away with the back of her fist.

"Just cry, damn it. You do need to catch up. My mama always said tears washed the poison from your soul."

She bit her lower lip and shook her head. She'd cried enough for one day.

And she was so tired. Tired of carrying the burden of fear, of regret, of loss alone.

But she wasn't alone. Not anymore. She looked into Dillon's patient eyes. He was back. He was there. Listening.

She drew a deep breath. She needed to explain to someone. She needed to explain to him. "I just wanted Amanda to have what I had growing up, that's all."

He didn't say anything, just looked at her with those steady dark eyes and waited for her to go on.

"I had a wonderful childhood. A mother and father who loved me. Took care of me. Kept me safe. I wanted that for her."

Words tumbled from her lips. "But she'll never have that kind of childhood. She'll never feel safe. She'll never look at the world as a good place again. And I can't fix it. Nothing I do will change what she saw. Nothing I do will make things right again. Some mother I turned out to be...." Her voice trailed off in a hoarse whisper, emotion choking her.

Dillon brushed his thumb over her cheekbone, wiping away the tear. His touch, so gentle, so intimate, seared her skin. The scent of soap and musk and male reached into her chilled blood like heated tendrils. She fought the urge to lean against him, to soak up his heat, his strength.

"You're a hell of a mother, Jacqueline." His drawl washed over her like a slow river over rocks. "And a hell of a woman."

She raised her chin and looked into his eyes. His gaze held hers. The tenderness was still there. But now it was joined by something else. Something deep and hot and piercing.

Yearning seeped through her and penetrated the very marrow of her bones. She should pull back. She should push his hand away. She should squelch the wave of longing building inside her before it washed away her common sense. But she couldn't.

More than that. She wouldn't.

She wanted his touch. She wanted his warmth. She wanted to cry out, to burrow into his arms and feel safe and secure and at peace if only for a moment. She was tired of trying to do it alone. She couldn't do it alone anymore.

He traced the line of her jaw with his thumb, heat chasing his feather touch. His eyes burned into hers.

She reached up, tangling her fingers in the waves of his hair. Locking her hands behind his neck, she drew his mouth down against hers. Hard. Demanding. The way she wanted his kiss. The way she needed it. To fill her. To chase away the fear. To make her feel less alone.

Fire laced her blood. Painful in its intensity. Like the hot needles of agony as a cold-numbed limb wakes from a deep chill.

His lips crushed hers. His tongue entered her mouth, probing, claiming. His arms encircled her waist, crushing her against his long, hard body.

A whimper rose from her lips.

This was stupid. Foolhardy with a daughter in danger and a killer on their heels. But she couldn't bring herself to pull back. Couldn't force herself to break the kiss. Because, foolhardy or not, she needed it.

Right now she needed his kiss more than she needed oxygen.

Heat whipped through Dillon's veins and pooled in his groin. It had been so long since he'd kissed a woman. So long since he'd felt a woman in his arms.

And what a woman.

He luxuriated in the softness of her body, the flavor of her lips. Like roasted honey. Sweet. Hot. Delicious.

And he didn't have a right to any of it.

Drawing in a breath of resolve, he broke the kiss. He reached behind his neck, clasped her hands in his and brought her fingers to his lips. "I'm sorry."

She stared up at him, her eyes large, luminous. "There's nothing to be sorry for. I kissed you, not the other way around. And I'm not sorry. I needed it."

He closed his eyes. "Damn, I needed it, too." But that didn't change anything. Jacqueline wasn't the type of woman who kissed just for the fun of it. A kiss meant something to her. Something far beyond simple lust.

And kissing her meant something to him, as well. Kissing Jacqueline was a promise. A promise for the future.

A promise he knew damn well he couldn't keep.

He'd broken enough promises to Jacqueline. He wouldn't—couldn't make any more that he couldn't keep. "But it wasn't a good idea. For a lot of reasons. You know that, and I know that."

She nodded. "Yes." Her tone was matter-of-fact, but her eyes held naked longing.

And he drank in that longing with an unquenchable thirst.

JACQUELINE HUNCHED DOWN at the kitchen sink and tried to concentrate on the paring knife flashing in her hand, peeling the potato into the garbage disposal. She'd thought that a normal task like helping Dillon prepare dinner would settle her mind. Make her feel more grounded. Make her focus on something besides the memory of his lips pressed to hers, his arms crushing her against his strong chest. But it wasn't working.

For the millionth time, her knife stilled. Her gaze shifted away from her work, wandered past Amanda sitting at the table coloring, and came to rest on Dillon.

He stood at the opposite end of the kitchen, next to the stove. His back to her, he diced onions with a chef's knife. His muscles moved smoothly under his denim shirt with each chop. The bright overhead kitchen lights glinted off the waves in his black hair.

Yearning strained in her chest. She'd been alone for so long. Alone with the responsibility of raising her daughter. Alone with the fear of losing her. Even before her divorce, Mark had been gone so much he was more like a visitor than a husband.

She drew in a fortifying breath. The eye-watering odor of onion saturated the air and stung her sinuses. This afternoon, when Dillon had dried her tears, when he'd listened to her fears for Amanda, when he'd taken her into his arms and kissed her, she hadn't been alone. For a moment she'd known what it was like to be cared for, to be safe.

But Dillon was right. They couldn't let it happen again.

His presence in her life was temporary. After this ordeal was over and Amanda was safe, he would go on with his crusade for justice. And she'd go back to her life. Raising Amanda. Helping her little girl overcome the hell she'd lived through.

That's the way it would be.

He could help ease her burden for now, but she mustn't let herself get too involved with him. No more crying on his shoulder. No more kissing. She didn't need a broken heart to add to her problems. Getting Amanda back up and running was going to be tough enough, if—no, *when* they escaped from this nightmare.

She tore her gaze from Dillon's back and focused on her daughter. Her heart lurched at the listless way the crayon dangled from her little fingers. When Amanda had awakened from her nap she had seemed brighter. But now she seemed to be hitting a spell of sadness again. Apparently coloring wasn't enough of a distraction. "Punkin, do you want to watch cartoons on TV instead of coloring?"

Amanda's nod was almost imperceptible. Jacqueline set the paring knife and potato next to the sink, wiped her hands on a paper towel and crossed the room to the small television perched on the kitchen counter. She snapped it on.

The polished voice of the local news anchorwoman rose from the box, her bleached-blond smile beaming from the screen. Jacqueline reached for the knob to change the channel.

"My daddy knows her." Amanda's thin voice rose above the television.

Jacqueline glanced up at her daughter. Her little finger pointed to the television. On the screen, the anchorwoman smiled a plastic smile and giggled at the sports guy's joke.

At Amanda's coo of a voice Dillon turned from his task. He looked to Jacqueline, his black brows arched in a silent question.

"She interviewed Mark," Jacqueline explained. "Jancy Brock. An in-depth look at a witness doing the right thing despite the threat to his safety."

A bitter taste rose in her mouth. Mark had been so excited, one would have thought he'd won a trip around the world instead of a mention on the local news. He'd thrown a party at the pub the night his interview aired.

Amanda looked straight at Dillon. "He talked to that lady on TV. And she wanted to talk to him again, too. He is important, my daddy."

A pain shot through Jacqueline at Amanda's use of the present tense to describe Mark. As if she didn't realize he was dead. Or refused to acknowledge it.

If Dillon recognized her selection of tense, he gave no outward sign. He set his chef's knife on the cutting board and leaned back against the counter, giving Amanda his full attention. "Yes, he was. Very important."

Amanda narrowed her eyes. Her hand found its way into her hair, twisting a shank into a tight rope. "More important than you?"

Jacqueline noted the challenge edging her little girl's voice. The tone Amanda had used often to defend Mark's absences at key moments like her seventh birthday party. Amanda had been so disappointed that day, but she wouldn't say one bad word about her daddy. And she wouldn't stand for anyone else to voice their disapproval, either. As if she was afraid he'd never want to see her again if she became angry with him.

Dillon nodded. "Much more important than me. Your daddy was a witness. I wouldn't even have a job if it wasn't for witnesses like your daddy."

She bit her lower lip, the worry lines slashed across her little brow breaking Jacqueline's heart. "He's brave, isn't he?"

Once again, Dillon nodded. "Very brave. Your daddy was very brave."

"Brave like you?"

"Thank you, darlin', but your daddy was far braver than me."

Amanda shook her head vigorously. "He's brave like you."

Jacqueline's throat closed. Amanda was so vulnerable. She wanted so desperately to rely on someone to protect her. She prayed that Dillon would recognize her compliment for what it was—Amanda's attempt to reassure herself that he was brave enough, strong enough to keep her safe.

Slowly he straightened himself from the counter and walked across the room toward Amanda. He squatted in front of her chair and looked deep into her eyes. "I may not be as brave as your daddy, sweetheart, but I'm a darn sight braver than any bad guys out there. That you can count on. You're safe with me."

"And Mommy?"

"Your mommy's safe, too." He gently plucked the twisted rope of hair from her chubby fingers and enveloped her hands in his large palms. "You don't have to worry."

Amanda leaned forward, stretched her arms around his neck and rested her head on his shoulder. A shuddering sigh escaped her lips. A sigh of relief. A sigh of thanks. A sigh of trust.

Jacqueline's eyes burned.

After the years of Mark's neglect, her little girl was starved for a father figure, and now it seemed she had chosen Dillon.

Jacqueline had been so concerned with the dangers Dillon had posed to her own emotional well-being, she'd never considered his effect on Amanda. What would happen when this nightmare was over? When they returned to their lives and Dillon returned to his?

Her poor little girl had been through enough. Enough danger, enough fear, enough heartbreak. She had already lost her father; she didn't need to let Dillon into her heart and then lose him, too.

Jacqueline didn't know what she could say or do,

but she had to do something. She had to protect her little girl's heart.

And she had to protect her own heart, too.

She opened her mouth to speak just as the doorbell's chime echoed through the little house.

Chapter Eight

The doorbell's chime vibrated through the still air. Dillon straightened, a jolt of adrenaline rushing into his bloodstream. He wasn't expecting anyone. Door-to-door salesmen and Girl Scouts peddling cookies didn't generally make it out to his remote home. So who the hell was at his door?

Jacqueline turned her pale face up to look at him, her eyes round with fear. "It can't be—"

"Swain?" he finished for her. "I doubt he would ring the bell."

"Then who?"

Once again Dillon searched his mind. Once again he came up empty. "I don't know."

Amanda turned her wide blue eyes on him. Although her face was pinched with fear, there was something soft in her eyes. Something that could only be trust.

He clenched his jaw. He damn well wouldn't let her down. "I'm sure it's nothing. But just in case, I want you to go into the bedroom and close the door. And don't turn on the light."

Jacqueline gave him a nod and rose from her chair.

In a flash, Amanda was beside her, both arms wrapped around her mother's leg as if she was holding on for dear life. A second later they had disappeared down the short hallway. The bedroom door clunked softly as it closed behind them.

The doorbell rang again.

Whoever was out there wasn't going away. Dillon made a quick inspection of the kitchen, looking for anything out of place. Anything that would give Jacqueline's and Amanda's presence away.

Jacqueline had done a good job of corralling their belongings in the bedroom where they could be hidden away from anyone who happened to stop by. But—

He reached down under the table and picked up Amanda's stuffed horse. Apparently the little girl had dropped the well-worn critter when she'd wrapped herself around her mother's leg. Dillon stashed the horse in the closest cupboard and strode into the living room.

He swept the room with his gaze. Satisfied that nothing in the house would give them away, Dillon retrieved the Defender from his locked desk drawer and tucked it in the waistband of his jeans. The nickel plate pressed reassuringly against his back, cool even through his denim shirt.

If only he could see the alcove of the stoop from the picture window. Then he'd know who waited at the door. He wouldn't have to open the damned thing blind. As soon as he dealt with his visitor, he'd install a peephole in the door. He reached for the doorknob. He pulled the door open a crack, his free hand poised over the gun.

"Hey, Dillon." Kit Ashner peered up at him.

"Kit?" What in hell was Kit doing here? Although he spent most of his waking life with her and the other task force members at the office, none of them had ever visited his house before. And he'd never visited theirs. A cold chill slid up his backbone. He rested his fingers on the Defender's grip.

"What? You have a lot of crime in this neighborhood suddenly? Or are you shacked up with some woman in there? Open the door and let me in, damn it."

Normally Kit's brashness brought a smile to his face. But not tonight. Her sudden unexplained appearance didn't amuse him. Not at all. What was she up to?

Only one way to find out. He unfastened the safety chain and opened the door.

Kit bulled past him and into the house, her caramel-colored eyes searching the room like a damned storm trooper. It was as if she was looking for something out of place. Something that belonged to a little girl or her mother. "Nice place you've got here. Obviously the same decorator that did your office. Spartan yet cluttered. Unique, but truly you."

"What do you want, Kit?" he asked in his gruffest voice.

She raised an eyebrow as if she was offended at his tone. Good. Maybe she'd gotten the idea that he didn't want her here. Maybe she'd leave.

"Are you waiting for a hot date or something? Want me gone before she gets here?" She tilted her head and made a face. "Naw. Not a hot date. Not you. Your social life is even more pitiful than mine."

"Kit. Get to the point. Why are you here?"

"Don't get your shorts in a bundle. I'm getting to it." She crossed the room, plunked herself on the couch and slapped the cushion next to her. "We've got to talk, Reese."

He frowned at her and stayed rooted to his spot, keeping his body angled so she couldn't see the Defender. "Then talk, Kit. I have a lot of work to do." Like digging into that box of personnel files. Maybe Kit's file would shed some light on her reason for being here tonight. Maybe she was the one with the connection to Swain, and she'd stopped by to fish for Amanda's whereabouts.

"Work. That's why I'm here. I couldn't talk to you at the office today, so I thought I'd drop by."

"What's wrong with your telephone?"

She dismissed his question with a wave of her hand. "I prefer personal contact. What did you find out from the little girl?"

He'd been so intent on protecting Amanda from the task force, he'd almost forgotten he was supposed to at least appear to be working *with* them on this case. He shrugged. "Not much. She hasn't been doing a lot of talking."

"Trauma?"

He nodded.

"Where did you stash her? We need to get a child psychologist out to talk to her right away."

Cold chills coursed down his spine. Maybe her inquiry was innocent, but he didn't want to take the chance that it wasn't. "I'll take care of it."

"And a police guard. Who do you have watching

her? No one downtown seems to know anything about her."

"Like I said, I'll take care of it."

Kit frowned, and if Dillon wasn't mistaken, her eyes seemed to narrow with suspicion. "When did you become the Lone Ranger?"

"What?"

"You've got to admit the way you've cut yourself off from the office in this case is a little extreme. No one seems to know where you've hidden the girl and her mother. And now you won't let me bring in a psychologist. What's going on here, Reese?"

He had to come up with something to get Kit off the trail, and he had to do it fast. "I don't want her testimony compromised. With a girl that young, after she's talked to two dozen 'experts,' I won't know if she's telling me what *she* remembers or what she's picked up from all the leading questions."

"But you can't just keep her shuttered away until the trial."

"Why not?"

"Because the task force is supposed to be a team, damn it. We're supposed to work together. With you and Harrington grabbing the spotlight, Britt and I are no more than glorified support staff." Eyes flashing at the injustice, Kit raised her chin and clenched her fists like a suffragette spoiling for a fight.

Dillon nodded his head knowingly. "Is that what this is about to you, Kit? A share of the spotlight?"

Temper hovered over Kit like a storm cloud. "Don't be an ass, Reese. I want Swain off the streets just as much as you do."

It was a good save, he'd have to give her that. But

was her guilty conscience a result of her ambition, or did it have more to do with a bargain with Swain? Either way, he couldn't let her find out the little girl she was looking for was huddled in the next room. He had to get her out of here. *Pronto*. "Well, don't worry. When Swain comes to trial again, I'll shed so much of the credit for his conviction your way you won't have any cause to complain. Now, let me get back to work."

Kit shot him a glare and rose from the couch. "Fine. I'll tell the gang you have everything under control. For now."

"The gang?"

"The task force. I was sent as the ambassador. This visit wasn't just my idea, you know."

Dillon's gut clenched. If the whole task force was behind Kit's plan to check out his house, any one of the district attorneys or police detectives could have initiated the idea. Any one of the task force members could be waiting for Kit to report back about her visit, ready to forward Amanda's whereabouts to Swain. "How did you get so lucky, Ms. Ambassador? Just whose idea was your little visit?"

She shrugged and breezed past him on her way to the door. "I live on this side of town. I guess everyone figured it wouldn't be out of my way to stop." She wrapped her scarf around her neck and chin and pulled open the door. A wave of cold air invaded the room. Pausing on the stoop, she glanced at him over her shoulder. "Will you be in the office on Monday?"

"I don't know. Tell Fitz I'll be in touch with him." He closed the door soundly behind her and slid the lock home. She hadn't seemed to notice he wasn't in the house alone. That the child she was looking for was only a closed door away. He should be relieved. But somehow, he couldn't quite manage it. Muscles cramped in his neck and shoulders. And once again his fingers found the Defender's grip.

He walked to the living-room window and peered out between the slats of the blinds just in time to see Kit duck into her car. The engine purred to life. A minute later, the road was deserted.

But the tension in his neck hadn't diminished. He stared out the window for a few more minutes, not sure what he was waiting for. But nothing happened.

Not a thing.

He let the blind slat fall back into place.

After retrieving Amanda's stuffed horse from the cupboard, he strode into the hall. He stopped outside the bedroom door, raised his fist and knocked gently. "Jacqueline?"

The knob turned and the door fell away from his hand. Suddenly two sets of blue eyes looked up at him out of the darkness of the room. So round. So frightened.

Tension gripped his neck and shoulders like an iron hand.

Kit was long gone. From all appearances, his house was as safe a hiding place for Jacqueline and Amanda as it had been before Kit's visit.

Then why couldn't he shake this damned ominous chill?

Because he couldn't be sure. And looking into Jacqueline's and Amanda's trusting blue eyes, he knew he couldn't take the chance. "We have to get out of here."

JACQUELINE SET her paisley suitcases on the floor of the living room and pulled Amanda as close as their bulky parkas would allow.

Dillon stood at his desk, stuffing legal folders into his briefcase. He drew his gun out of a desk drawer. Its silver barrel reflected the overhead lights with a cold gleam. He shoved it into the pocket of his black duster. "Ready?"

She nodded, not willing to trust her voice.

Judging from the obvious concern in his eyes, her silence hadn't fooled Dillon. "You okay?"

Amanda's eyes snapped to her face, searching for reassurance, for strength.

Jacqueline forced a smile to her lips. She didn't want to broadcast her fear to Amanda. Besides, there was no reason to be afraid. They were leaving only as a precaution. That was what Dillon had explained before she packed their belongings and bundled Amanda and herself for the outside weather. Only a precaution. No reason to panic. She tried her best to lighten her voice, as if their evacuation was nothing more than a mini holiday. "Ready as I'll ever be. Where are we going?"

"To a motel. Someplace on the other side of town." Locking his briefcase and leaving it on the desktop, he scooped up the suitcases and headed for the kitchen. "I'll load these in the car and take a look around. Wait until I get back."

Jacqueline took Amanda's mittened hand in her own and glanced toward the picture window that looked out on the road. Could someone be out there? Watching? Waiting? A tremor seized her hands. She tried her best to calm herself. As Dillon had said, it might be nothing. Kit Ashner probably didn't have a clue they were in the house. She probably wasn't Swain's source. Most likely, they were abandoning Dillon's house for no reason other than paranoia.

But paranoia being what it was, she had to check.

She stepped toward the edge of the picture window. Clinging to the window's frame so she couldn't be seen from the outside, she split the closed slats of the blind with her fingers and peered through.

The full moon cast a gentle glow over banks of snow. The white bark of a clump of birch trees shimmered with frost. Behind the silvery branches the forest loomed, dark and foreboding and wild. But the road seemed deserted. Safe. No one watching. No one waiting. A sigh of relief escaped her lips.

Then she saw it. A spark. And then a reddish glow from the edge of the forest.

The glow of a lighted cigarette.

A scream lodged in Jacqueline's throat. She covered her mouth with a hand.

Could it be Swain?

She withdrew her other hand from the blind and stepped back from the window. Her breath raged in her ears, its roar competing with the drumming of her heart. Inhaling deeply, she tried to slow her breathing. Tried not to panic Amanda.

The kitchen door creaked and Dillon's booted footstep thunked on the floor.

Dillon. She had to tell Dillon.

As calmly as she could manage, she lifted Amanda in her arms and walked into the kitchen.

When Dillon spotted her, his eyes grew wide. "What happened?"

"Someone's outside. On the edge of the woods."

Cursing under his breath, he strode past her, parted the blind slats as she had, and looked out. "Damn."

That single word chilled Jacqueline to the bone. "Is it Swain?"

"I don't know for sure. But I can't imagine who else it could be." He let the blind fall back into place. The sharp planes of his face were hard, stark. His black brows slanted low over his eyes. "He's probably waiting for me to usher you out to the car."

Dread sank into Jacqueline like sharp teeth into helpless prey. Amanda tensed in her arms. "What are we going to do?"

"Let him wait. Come on." After grabbing his briefcase from the desktop, Dillon spun and strode into the dark bedroom with Jacqueline and Amanda on his heels. He crossed to the double hung window that looked out on the backyard. He pulled up the blind, unlocked the latch and slid the sash and storm window open.

Cold air rushed into the room, slapping Jacqueline's heated cheeks and clearing her mind.

Dillon tossed his briefcase out the window and turned to Jacqueline. "The Meinholz farm isn't but a couple of miles through the forest. By the time Swain figures out we're no longer in the house, we'll be long gone. If everything works out."

Please God, let everything work out.

Dillon climbed out the window and reached back

through. The moon's glow illuminated the planes of his face. Despite the tension evident in the lines around his eyes and mouth, he gave Amanda a smile and a wink. "Come on, darlin'. I'll bet you never left the house through a window before."

Drawing a deep breath, Jacqueline placed her baby in his arms. Amanda wrapped one arm around his neck and clung.

"Now I have to help your mommy, darlin'." He pried her arm loose and set her in the snow next to him.

Amanda looked up at Jacqueline. Trembling visibly, she bit her bottom lip and folded both arms around Dorsey.

Jacqueline lowered herself out the window. Dillon's hands closed around her waist, so strong, so steady. He guided her to the snowdrift below.

The outside air was cold, deathly still, and spiked with the scent of burning wood. A dog barked in the distance, the sound brittle in the cold air.

Dillon lifted Amanda back into his arms. Locking her hands around his neck, she encompassed her stuffed pony in the hug and buried her face in his shoulder.

With a tilt of his head Dillon motioned Jacqueline to follow. He spun and strode off through the snow.

Jacqueline grabbed the briefcase from the snow and followed, struggling to keep up with his rolling stride. Snow crunched under her boots, the sound loud as firecrackers in the still night.

Please, God, don't let Swain hear.

They ran across the backyard and plunged into the forest. Moonlight filtered through the naked branches, puddling in pools on the snow. Dillon picked and dodged between trees and brush. His stride didn't hesitate. Didn't slow. His shoulders blocked her view of the path ahead.

She focused on the ground in front of her. Concentrated on placing one foot in front of the other. The snow slipped under her boots, icy from the repeated freeze and thaw of late winter. She grasped a bush to retain her balance. Wild raspberry. The thorns snagged the fabric of her glove and dug into her hand.

She straightened and moved on, struggling to keep up with Dillon. A branch cracked under her foot. The pop of sound cut the quiet night.

She held her breath.

Dillon stopped and glanced over his shoulder. His dark gaze rested on her for a heartbeat, then scanned the naked branches, the snow dappled with moonlight. He dipped his hand into the pocket of his duster and withdrew the gun. They stood dead still. Waiting for the snap of a twig. A rustle of movement. Some warning that Swain was near.

Stalking.

Jacqueline drew a breath of icy air into her lungs. If he hadn't already heard them moving through the trees, he would surely hear the pounding of her heart.

An owl's screech splintered the silence.

Nothing. Nothing but an owl.

Ahead of her, Dillon resumed his ground-eating pace. Amanda bounced on his hip with each stride. Her stuffed horsey bobbed in the circle of her arms, its plastic eyes reflecting the light of the moon.

Jacqueline struggled to keep up. The cold air froze

the inside of her nostrils with each breath, making her throat and ears ache.

She pushed on.

They had to hurry. They had to put distance between them and Swain. No amount of distance would be enough.

Dillon halted.

Jacqueline peeked around his shoulders to see why. They had reached the crest of a hill. Still heavily wooded, the ground sloped away severely in front of him.

The snow on the slope reflected patches of moonlight like polished glass, stretches of it packed into white ice. It would be treacherous. Slow going. But they had no choice but to go forward. They certainly couldn't turn back.

"Be careful, Dillon," she whispered.

He nodded. Grasping tree trunks with his free hand to keep from falling, Dillon started down the slope.

They inched down through the trees. Despite the chill in the air, sweat trickled down Jacqueline's back and between her breasts. At this pace, if Swain had discovered their escape, he could catch up to them easily. Clinging to the thin trunk of a sapling, she turned and glanced up the hill.

Branches clawed into the moonlight. Shadows shimmered in and out of the trees like ghosts. Could one of those shadows be Swain? Could he have already found them?

She turned back to the trail in front of her and hurried to catch up to Dillon and Amanda. The sky seemed to glow brighter through the trees ahead. A field. Maybe a farm.

A place they could call for help.

Finally they reached the edge of the forest. A cornfield stretched in front of them. Stubble from last year's crop protruded through the snow in rough rows. All open.

No cover.

Beyond the field and across a country road, an old red cow barn nestled in the hillside.

"Is that the farm you were talking about?"

Dillon nodded. "First we're going to have to get across the field. We're going to stick out like a tin roof on a sunny day against that snow."

He was right. The moonlight that had assisted them in making their way through the shadows of the forest would now highlight them against the snow as effectively as a spotlight's glare.

"Couldn't we just stay in the trees? There's bound to be another farm or house."

He shook his head. "That's the problem. There isn't. Not for several miles. The Meinholz place is our best bet." He shifted Amanda to his other arm. "We're going to have to run for it."

Jacqueline pushed from her mind the image of their backs illuminated like targets against the white snow, and nodded. "I'm right behind you."

"If you hear gunshots, I want you to run in a zig-zag."

Jacqueline swallowed the hard lump of fear in her throat. "Zigzag, got it."

"And Jacqueline?"

"Yes?"

"We're going to be okay." He rested a hand on

her shoulder, a reassuring smile lifting the corners of his lips.

Even though she knew he couldn't promise anything of the sort, at that moment she believed him. With all her heart. "I know. Now run. I'm right behind you."

After one last smile, Dillon ran out of the forest's shadow in the direction of the barn. Bobbing with each stride, Amanda held on tight.

Jacqueline set out after them. Her boots crunched over bits of frozen cornstalk. She skidded on the icy snow. She caught her balance before falling and pushed on.

Ahead of her, Dillon settled into a smooth, ground-covering stride, his black duster furling out behind him like a cape, stark against the white snow.

By the time they'd reached the halfway mark, Jacqueline's lungs burned and her head ached. The briefcase in her fist was as heavy as if it were made of solid lead. But she couldn't slow down, couldn't let up. Stopping now might make the difference between life and death. They had to reach the farm. She pushed herself faster.

The red barn loomed closer. Jacqueline glanced over her shoulder as she ran. A shape hovered on the edge of the field. Dark against the snow's white glow. An evergreen tree?

The shape moved. *A man.*

"Dillon."

Up ahead, Dillon lengthened his stride in an all-out sprint. He neared the edge of the field and the ditch by the side of the country road.

Please, God, let him reach cover before—

A crack split the air.

Dillon dived into the ditch.

Jacqueline's heart lurched into her throat. *Her baby.*

Chapter Nine

Jacqueline scrambled across the snow. She had to get to her little girl. She had to.

She raced over the edge of the ditch and into a tangle of sumac. The gnarled branches tore at her hair and parka like frantic fingers. Dillon's hand closed over her upper arm.

"Amanda! Is Amanda—" She scrambled to free herself from the branches.

"She's all right."

Jacqueline exhaled. Tears flooded her eyes and cascaded down her cheeks.

Amanda was safe.

She lifted her daughter from Dillon's arms, pressing her sweet trembling body against her breast. She kissed her tear-streaked little face. So warm. So alive. *Thank God.* Amanda was safe.

Dillon took the briefcase from her clenched fist. He stared at his arm and then back at Amanda. His face drained of color.

She followed the direction of his gaze. The shoulder of Dillon's duster was torn and frayed. A moment passed before Jacqueline realized what she was seeing. A bullet hole. The bullet had just missed Dillon. And her little girl.

Her heart slammed so hard against her ribs that shock waves turned her stomach.

Dillon reached into his pocket and pulled out his gun. "Meinholz has a phone in the barn. Take Amanda and run."

"Without you?" Panic crashed through her.

He gave a curt nod, his focus on the lip of the ditch. "I'm going to stay here and see if I can slow Swain down."

He was planning to confront Swain. Alone. "*No*. Come with us. We—"

"I'll be right behind you. As soon as I make sure Swain isn't behind you, too." He met her eyes for a whisper of a second before turning his eyes back to the flat field stretching beyond the lip of the ditch. "If I'm firing at him, he's going to have to take cover. He won't be able to get a shot off while you're running to the barn."

Turning her back on the open stretch of field where Swain lurked, she glanced up the slope to the white-fenced cow yard, to the barn beyond. Only about half a football field. Half a football field and she'd be able to put a cement wall between her little girl and Swain. Half a football field and she'd be able to call for help.

She spun back to Dillon. A cold tremor started deep in the pit of her stomach. "Come with us. He could shoot you. He could—"

He grasped her shoulder, his grip firm, reassuring. "I know who I'm dealing with, Jacqueline. This is our best bet. I'll be right behind you. I promise."

She looked into his dark eyes. She had no choice but to believe him. She had to get Amanda to that barn. She had to call for help. "I'll hold you to that promise."

A smile curved the corners of his mouth. "I expected you would." The smile disappeared. He nodded toward the farm. "The telephone is near the front of the barn."

Jacqueline nodded. "I'll find it."

"Just call 911. Tell the operator you're here with me." He turned back to the cornfield. His eyes narrowed to slits. "When I say move, I want you to run for the door of that barn as fast as you can."

Jacqueline heaved Amanda higher on her hip. "Hold on tight, baby."

Amanda tightened her grip. She laid her little head on Jacqueline's shoulder, her warm breath fanning her neck.

Dillon positioned the gun in front of him. He rose from the ditch. *"Move."*

Jacqueline straightened to her feet and lunged up the slope to the road. She raced over the road, her boots clattering on the hard pavement.

A shot from Dillon's gun split the night. And another.

She bolted through the ditch on the other side of the road and up the slope. Reaching the white fence, she ducked between the boards.

She straightened and plunged ahead into the cow yard. Her feet broke through the icy crust on the surface and sank into thick, muddy sludge. She trudged through the sludge. One foot after the other. Cold seeped into her boots, making her feet ache.

Shots rang in her ears.

Amanda whimpered.

"It's okay, baby. We're almost there." She fought on. The mud sucked at her boots and oozed over her ankles.

Finally she reached the huge sliding door of the barn. She grabbed the steel handle, her gloves snagging on the door's rough wood. She gave the door a push.

It didn't budge.

"Hold on tight, Amanda. I need both hands to push open this door."

Balancing on her hip, her daughter hugged her neck tightly. She let go of Amanda and grasped the handle with both hands. Bracing herself against the stone wall, she shoved the door with all her strength.

The door runner creaked its protest. Slowly it slid open. One foot. Two feet.

She slipped into the darkness.

Oppressive heat and humidity cloaked her like a thick blanket. The sharp odor of cow manure filled her mouth and nostrils and clogged in her throat. Dark shapes surrounded them in the darkness.

As her eyes adjusted, she could see a row of cow rumps framing both sides of the aisle where she and Amanda stood. The closest were craning their necks to peer at them with big shiny eyes. The low rumble of grinding teeth churned through the barn like the constant buzz from a beehive.

Amanda gasped. She squeezed Jacqueline's neck tighter and buried her eyes in the hood of her parka.

"It's okay, punkin. Cows like people. They won't hurt us." Jacqueline sized up the beasts. Or would they? When it came right down to it, she didn't know what cows would do. Although she'd lived in Wisconsin much of her life, she hadn't seen cows up close until now.

The muffled report of a gunshot infiltrated the barn.

Jacqueline's heart lurched.

She had something a lot more dangerous to be frightened of than cows. She had to find a telephone. And she had to do it now.

Dillon had said the phone was at the front of the barn. But which end was considered the front? She peered through the shadows on either side of the door. No sign of a phone. It must be on the other end.

Walking down the center aisle, she strained her eyes to see through the darkness ahead of her. Moonlight glowed through a window up ahead. She focused on the light and walked toward it. Sweat beaded on her forehead and drenched the tendrils of hair framing her face. The cows shifted and stomped in their stanchions.

Reaching the other end of the barn, she dodged around a snowmobile parked in the middle of the aisle. An old telephone was attached to the wall under the window. She grabbed the grungy receiver off the hook and raised it to her ear.

No dial tone.

Dread trickled down her spine. Cradling the receiver in the crook of her neck, she pressed the hook several times. Still nothing.

The phone was dead.

The house. Would the phone in the house also be

dead? She had to find out. She had to get to the house. She wiped the grime from the windowpane with her gloved fingers and peered out into the night.

A farm light cast an orange glow over the driveway and yard. No fences stood in her way. Nothing to slow her down. She could easily run across the open space to the house.

The farmhouse's hulking shape loomed at the edge of the hill. Dark. Seemingly deserted. Even if the Meinholzes had gone to bed early, the sound of gunfire echoing through the valley surely would have awakened them. The family must not be home.

Which meant the house was likely locked.

Defeat landed like a hard kick to her stomach. She would never be able to break in to the house and find a telephone in time. And for all she knew, the phone in the house was dead, too.

She thought of Dillon hunched down in the ditch, trying to keep Swain at bay until help arrived. But with no phone, help wouldn't arrive. How long before Dillon would run out of bullets? How long before Swain shot him down?

She turned away from the window. Stepping back into the barn's murky darkness, she almost ran into the front runner of the snowmobile.

The snowmobile.

She set Amanda on the padded seat and knelt next to the machine. It was newer than the model she'd driven at Mark's friend's cabin up north, but the important things were still the same. The accelerator. The steering.

And the key was in the ignition.

They just might get out of this yet. They could

just hop on the snowmobile and head over the crest of the hill. Away from Swain. Away from danger.

But first she had to go back and get Dillon.

She took Amanda's hand and led her to the corner of the barn. Hollowing out a small cave among old milking equipment and pieces of lawn furniture, she checked for signs of mice and other vermin. Thankfully the Meinholz family kept a clean barn. She nestled Amanda into the protective little shelter. "I want you to stay here and hide, sweetheart. After I go out and pick up Mr. Reese, I'm going to take you for a snowmobile ride."

DILLON LIFTED HIS HEAD and peered over the lip of the ditch. The cornfield stretched in front of him, shorn stalks jutting up out of the snow like stubble on a chin. He narrowed his eyes and strained to catch a glimpse of movement. A whisper of sound.

Somewhere out there Swain bided his time. Or advanced. Or lined up Dillon in his sights. The cold, malevolent feel of his presence seemed to hang in the air like the late-winter chill.

Hell, Dillon probably wouldn't even be able to spot Swain until it was too late. After all, Swain was used to crawling on his belly, waiting for a clear shot at the enemy. He'd spent the better part of his life in special forces doing just that.

And Dillon was no soldier.

He could only hope Jacqueline had reached the telephone and had made the call. He could only hope that help was on its way. Because there was no telling how long he and the Defender could hold off a professional soldier like Swain.

Not very damn long, he'd be willing to bet.

A loud buzzing noise, like a bee on steroids, came from the direction of the barn. Dillon tore his attention from the cornfield. A dark object streaked across the snow. It skirted the orange glow of the farmyard light and headed straight for the ditch.

"What the hell?"

A snowmobile hurtled toward him. A single figure huddled on its seat. *Jacqueline.*

She was crazy, risking herself to save him. Plumb crazy.

And she just might be the bravest damn woman he'd ever met.

He swung back to the cornfield. If he'd spotted her, so had Swain. He had to keep the sharpshooter off balance. He couldn't give him time to line her up in his sights. Dillon rose on his knees on the edge of the ditch and fired several rounds into the cornfield.

Out of the corner of his eye he saw Jacqueline pilot the machine across the road and into the protection of the ditch.

Dillon scrambled to his feet and fired another round into the cornfield.

She slowed the snowmobile.

He mounted while it was still moving, swinging his leg over the seat, settling in behind Jacqueline. He circled one arm around her and fired his gun over his shoulder with the other as they sped back to the barn.

Once they reached the barn, it didn't take but a few seconds to pick up Amanda. Then they were off, over the hill. And away from Swain.

Chapter Ten

Jacqueline secured the towel over her wet hair in a turban and stepped out of the musty steaminess of the motel's bathroom. Even though she had scrubbed every inch of her skin, she could still smell the sharp tang of cow manure. It was as if the odor had penetrated her pores and melded with her very being.

At least once they had abandoned the snowmobile and rented a car they had been able to find a discount store open so she could buy some new clothing for herself and Amanda. Not that the blouses, jeans and boots she'd grabbed were any great shakes. But they were clean. And they carried that new-clothes smell instead of the stench of cow.

She walked from the bathroom and focused on her little girl still sitting on the multicolored bedspread, still staring blankly at the television screen. Frightened but alive. Funny how her mind could wander to trivial things such as the smell of cow manure after what they'd been through.

She sat on the bed next to Amanda. Her hand still trembled as she smoothed it over her little girl's damp-from-the-shower head. She unwrapped her own hair from the towel turban, letting her wet waves fall around her face. An unopened McDonald's bag perched on the bedside table. Neither she, Amanda, nor Dillon had touched their burgers. After the nightmare they'd survived tonight, she didn't have to wonder why. Jacqueline couldn't even imagine eating.

She had come so close. So close to losing her little girl. So close to losing Dillon. She shuddered with the memory.

Just a few short hours ago she had been primarily worried about protecting Amanda's heart. And her own. Worried her little girl would adopt Dillon as a father figure. Worried they both would be devastated when this ordeal was over and he walked out of their lives.

But Swain had changed all that.

He'd almost killed Amanda. Almost killed them all. Getting through this alive was the only thing Jacqueline could worry about. Everything else could wait until Swain was in prison and they were safe. Then she would have plenty of time to help heal her little girl's frayed emotions and broken heart.

And her own.

A key rattled in the lock, and even though she knew who was on the other side of the door, she tensed with the sound.

The door swung open and Dillon strode into the room. He offered her an exasperated look. A wavy lock of black hair slanted over his forehead, matching the ebony of his eyes.

A tingle stole over Jacqueline's skin at the sight of him. For a moment she just stared, drinking him in. They were alive and together and every moment, every glance, every breath seemed new and precious and so, so fleeting.

His eyebrows rose. A smile crooked one corner of his lips. "Hi, there."

"Hi." She couldn't help but smile. He probably thought she was crazy, staring at him this way. She was. But she couldn't help it. She couldn't pull her eyes away.

He stepped toward her, his gaze skimming over her damp, curling hair and discount-store clothes like a starving man eyeing a Thanksgiving turkey. "You look so clean and fresh and…beautiful."

Heat and pleasure flushed through her. It was such a simple statement, and yet it filled her with more pleasure than she'd felt in a long time. She liked the fact that he thought she looked beautiful. She liked it far too much. "Thank you."

"I should be the one thanking you."

"For what?"

"Picking me up with the snowmobile. It would have been safer for you and Amanda to take off in the other direction and leave me there." He shook his head, a spark of humor kindled in his dark eyes. Humor and something that resembled admiration. "That was plumb crazy. You know that, don't you? Crazy or brave."

He was right. It *had been* crazy. It sure hadn't been bravery. God knew she certainly wasn't brave.

She thought of Dillon firing at Swain from the ditch, holding off the killer while she took Amanda and ran for the barn. By staying in that ditch, Dillon had put his life on the line for Amanda and her. He'd vowed to protect Amanda with his life, and he'd kept that vow. And she was grateful.

More than grateful.

She folded her arms over her middle in an attempt to still the tremble in the pit of her stomach. Drawing herself up, she cocked her head and looked at him out of the corner of her eye. "I couldn't let you fend off Swain single-handedly and take all the glory, now, could I?"

A short laugh escaped his lips. "I figured it was something like that." The smile faded from his eyes, replaced by a look so intense it caused a shimmer to dance along her nerves. The heat of his gaze was palpable in the musty air of the motel room. "Whatever it was, thank you."

Her pulse beat faster. Her nerves pulled a little tighter. She knew she should thank him back, or toss him a chipper, easy "you're welcome," but the words caught in her throat.

She bit her bottom lip and let out the breath she didn't know she was holding. "Did you get in touch with Detective Mylinski?"

He frowned and paced across the room, back to business, the moment between them broken. "Not yet. He's not home. He's not downtown. I can't imagine where he could be. Unless he decided to take a trip to his fishing cabin in the middle of an investigation." He gave a short laugh as if that was unlikely and slid into a vinyl-upholstered chair near the door.

Cold foreboding niggled at the back of Jacqueline's neck. She pushed up from the bed, crossed the room to the table and lowered herself into a chair next to Dillon. "What if something's happened to him?"

Dillon's eyebrows turned down. "Like what?"

"What if Swain killed him?"

He dismissed her concern with a wave of his hand. "Swain has no reason to kill Mylinski. Mylinski's fine. He's probably just neck-deep in his investigation and hasn't checked his messages." He looked down at the contents of his briefcase spread across the table in front of him and began studying a file as if not giving her query a second thought. But she couldn't help noticing a note of tension in him that hadn't been there before.

"Have you found anything in the files?"

He paused a moment before raising his eyes to hers. "Not a thing."

Each folder on the table was labeled with a name. Dex Harrington. Kit Ashner. Britt Alcott. Dale Kearney. The members of the violent crime task force. One of those people had told Swain where he could find Mark. Where he could find Val.

And tonight, one of them had told him where he could find Amanda.

She spotted the name on the folder in front of Dillon. "Dex Harrington?" Mindful of Amanda lying on the bed behind her, she lowered her voice. "It was Kit Ashner who came to the house tonight."

"But she said she'd been sent by the task force, and I'm inclined to believe her. I've already been through the files I have on Kit. I didn't find anything to tie her to Swain. Not a damned thing."

Jacqueline shook her head. All she knew was that one moment Kit was at Dillon's door asking where

Amanda was, and the next moment Swain was waiting outside. "Just because there isn't an obvious connection in these files doesn't mean one doesn't exist."

"You're right. There may very well be something I don't know about."

"Have you found anything suspicious about Dex Harrington?"

"Not yet." He dropped the folder back into his briefcase. "Damn. If only I had the files I loaded into Mylinski's car back at the house."

"What's in those files?"

"More court records. Personal history, that sort of thing."

"Can Detective Mylinski bring those files to you?"

"If I could reach him." He leveled his black gaze on her, the fine lines around his mouth deep with tension. He lowered the volume of his voice even further. "Until I can get in touch with Mylinski, we sit tight and wait." His words sounded so ominous, so bleak.

"Wait for who?" Swain? Anxiety and frustration made her skin feel too tight.

"For Mylinski. He's likely checking out other leads as we speak. Eventually I *will* get in touch with him."

Unless he was dead. "And while we're waiting? What do you suggest we do? Twiddle our thumbs?" She caught herself just as her voice began to rise. She knew she was being irrational. Panicky. But somehow she couldn't help it. She stole a glance at Amanda over her shoulder.

"While we're waiting, I'll go through these files again. Line by line." His voice was calm, soothing. He leaned toward her and fixed her with an intense gaze. "If there's a connection to Swain in these files, I'll find it. I promise."

She dragged in a breath and tried to swallow the bitter bile of frustration. "I know." He was doing his best. If there was anything, anything at all in those files, he would find it.

But what if there wasn't anything in the files?

She looked back over her shoulder at Amanda. Her little girl hadn't moved. She still stared at the television as if she were in a trance. The colors from the flickering screen reflected on her face, turning her complexion blue, green, red.

Jacqueline clenched her fists. She had to do something to protect Amanda. She had to bring this ordeal to a close. Even if it meant her little girl would have to relive that horrible night.

She turned back to Dillon and swallowed around the lump in her throat. "I'm going to let you talk to her."

Dillon's eyes bored into Jacqueline for what seemed like hours. Probing. Assessing. Finally he tore his gaze from her and settled it on Amanda. "I'll make my questions as easy on her as I can."

Jacqueline nodded. She knew he would. She could see the caring in his eyes when he looked at her daughter. He wouldn't push her if she got upset. He wouldn't badger her. He would be careful. As careful as he could be. "Let her get some sleep first, if she can. You can talk to her tomorrow."

Dillon reached out and took her hand in his. The

pressure of his fingers was warm, reassuring. "We'll get through this, Jacqueline. We'll all get through this."

She gripped his hand and held on. She sure hoped he was right, because she couldn't bear to think what would happen if he wasn't.

THE LATE-MORNING SUN glowed weakly through the heavy curtains, lending the motel room its heat if not its light. Inhaling a breath of the musty air, Dillon spread paper and crayons on the scarred table in front of Amanda.

She automatically reached for the red crayon and began doodling a design. The tip of her pink little tongue peeked out between her lips in concentration.

Dillon lowered himself into the chair opposite her. He avoided glancing at Jacqueline standing behind her little girl, but he could feel her eyes on him. He could feel her apprehension. It wasn't that she didn't trust him. He knew she did. She damn well wouldn't be letting him talk to her little girl if she didn't. But she understood how rough this interview would be on her daughter. Remembering could be rough. And he didn't blame her for being scared for Amanda. Not one little bit.

He honed his attention in on the little girl. "Darlin', I want you to think back to the last night you were with your daddy. Do you remember that night?"

Amanda looked up from her drawing. She twisted in her chair to see her mother, to ask with a glance for permission to answer.

Jacqueline rested a reassuring hand on her little

girl's shoulder. "It's all right, punkin. Remember? This morning we talked about how it was all right for you to tell Mr. Reese everything." Her eyes rose and met his. "I trust him. Don't you?"

Dillon's mouth went dry. He knew she trusted him. She wouldn't be letting him talk to her little girl if she didn't. But hearing her say the words was another story altogether. It made him want to wish for a different life. It made him want to hope for a future. A future with Jacqueline and Amanda in it. A future he knew damn well couldn't be.

He wrested his eyes from Jacqueline's in time to see Amanda's small nod. "I was at Daddy's house watching *Little Mermaid*." Her voice was no louder than the coo of a mourning dove.

His mind snapped back to the present, back to the matter at hand. "Did your daddy get a phone call that night?" The caller ID installed in Mark Schettler's house showed him receiving a call from a pay phone on State Street less than an hour before his murder. Chances were whoever had placed that call had lured Mark to his death.

Unfortunately, Mylinski hadn't had any luck in locating a witness who might have noticed who used the phone at that time. And the lab had struck out trying to identify fingerprints on the telephone and the change inside. His last hope in identifying the caller rested on Amanda's memories. "Do you remember him getting a call, darlin'?"

She nodded her head. "He gets lots of calls. He's very important."

She was still using the present tense to describe her daddy. Poor kid. Even though she'd watched as he was killed, she couldn't face the fact that he was dead. And who the hell could blame her? Not him. Not for a second. He only wished he didn't have to make her remember. "Do you remember a call that night? Right before the two of you went to the brew pub?"

Her brow furrowed. "I didn't go to the brew pub. I watched *Little Mermaid*."

Obviously she didn't want to remember. "How about after you watched *Little Mermaid*? Didn't you go to the pub then?"

She shook her head.

He looked down at the paper she had stopped coloring. He didn't want to pressure her. Too much pressure and she might lock those memories away for good. He made his voice as gentle and casual as possible. "Remember? You called your mommy from the pub, and she came to get you. Didn't she find you under the desk in your daddy's office? That was a very smart place to hide."

Again she shook her head.

Jacqueline rubbed her hand over her daughter's shoulders. "You did a great job of hiding, sweetheart."

The little girl's fingers found her hair, twisting a shank in a nervous mannerism that had become familiar to him in the past few days. Her forehead puckered. "Daddy got a phone call from that lady. But then I went to sleep."

"What lady, Amanda? What lady called your daddy?"

"The lady on the TV."

His mind flashed to last night. Before they'd left

his house, Amanda had said that Mark had talked to the blond news anchor, Jancy Brock. And that she wanted to talk to him again. "Was it the lady you showed us on television last night? The lady that interviewed your daddy?"

She nodded. "She wants to talk to him on TV again. That's what daddy said. Daddy is real important."

Dillon met Jacqueline's eyes for a moment. The shock of discovery on her face matched the jolt that ran through him. Did Jancy Brock have some connection to Swain or a member of the task force? Did she lure Mark to the pub? Or did someone pretending to be the newswoman call Mark? "Is that why your daddy took you to the brew pub? To talk to the lady?"

"He was going to, but I fell asleep."

Dillon gave Amanda a sympathetic smile. He knew why she was insisting she hadn't gone to the brew pub. If she acknowledged that her memories weren't a dream, she'd have to face that Mark's murder was real, also.

A pain sliced through his chest. He'd give anything to not have to pull that memory and the pain associated with it out into the open. But his case depended on her remembering. And more important, her very life depended on it.

He'd worked on a case long ago where a young boy had insisted he remembered nothing about a crime. But when the child psychologist had asked him about a dream he'd had, the whole experience had rushed out.

"Amanda, after you fell asleep that night, did you have a dream about going to the brew pub?"

"Yes."

Bingo. Somehow he kept himself from leaning forward. "Can you tell me about your dream?"

"I dreamed I went to the pub. Daddy said I could talk to the lady. He said she would put me on TV, too."

Next to Dillon, Jacqueline bristled. He knew what she was thinking. After the lengths she went to to protect her daughter, to keep her out of the limelight and the line of fire, Mark had been willing to throw away all her efforts the night before his testimony. All for a moment in the spotlight. Damn fool. "Did you see the lady at the pub?"

"In my dream?"

"Yes."

Amanda shook her head. "She wasn't there. I was supposed to wait for her in daddy's office, but she never came."

"Did your daddy wait in his office, too?"

"No. He went down in the garden."

"The beer garden?"

She nodded. "But the lady wasn't down there, either."

"Was someone else down there?"

Amanda stared at a spot just to the left of Dillon, as if she was watching her memories play out on a movie screen. Her eyes grew wide. A slight whimper rose from her throat.

Next to him, Jacqueline drew in a sharp breath.

Dillon tensed. "Who was in the beer garden, Amanda?"

"That man. That man was down there."

Dillon's neck and shoulders began to throb. God forgive him, he had to make her say the words. "What man, Amanda?"

Still staring past him, Amanda's eyes widened with fear. "The man in the newspaper. The one daddy was gonna talk about in the court."

Hand shaking, Dillon withdrew a collection of photos from his briefcase and spread them over the tabletop. Six faces stared up at Amanda. Six mug shots. All of them in their thirties. All of them faces no little girl should ever have to see. "Is one of these men the one you saw in the beer garden with your daddy?"

She lowered her gaze to the table. Her round blue eyes filled with tears. Big drops rolled down her cheeks. She extended her index finger and pointed to one of the photos.

The photo of Buck Swain.

"He had a knife. He cut Daddy." She paused, a sob racking her body. "He killed my daddy."

Jacqueline folded her daughter in her arms, her own tears mingling with the little girl's.

Chapter Eleven

Dillon closed his aching eyes and stretched the muscles in his neck and shoulders. The day had passed, and night had slid into the motel room while he'd been studying the files.

He glanced up at the bed. Jacqueline sat with her back against the bed's headboard, her eyes closed. Her daughter curled under the covers next to her. Blessedly asleep. The little girl had spent most of the day crying in her mother's arms, and her round little cheeks were chapped pink from her tears.

Poor little darlin'. He'd hated making her relive her daddy's death. Hated making her realize the whole thing wasn't merely a bad dream. She didn't deserve this. Any of this.

And Jacqueline. The interview had shaken her, too. Shaken her to the core. What he'd seen in her eyes after Amanda had cried herself to sleep had worried him. Desperation. Despair. As if all her hope, all her fight had been washed away by her daughter's tears. Even now, leaning against the headboard, eyes closed, her beautiful face looked ashen and drawn. What he wouldn't give to erase the furrow of worry from her brow, to smooth the lines of tension framing her mouth.

What he wouldn't give…

Amanda had handed him the evidence he needed to put Swain away for good. He should feel elated. But he couldn't help worrying that the price was too high. Too high for the little girl. Too high for her mother.

And what had he really accomplished? Sure, he could now prove that Swain had murdered Mark Schettler, but Swain hadn't been arrested yet. He was still out there. Searching for them. Stalking them.

Looking to kill Amanda.

And Swain's mole was still in the task force, feeding him information. But if Dillon was lucky, the mole wouldn't be there for long.

He looked down at the paper in his hand just to make sure what he'd found wasn't merely the product of wishful thinking. The facts stared back at him, plain as fresh red paint on the broad side of a barn.

A connection.

He might not be able to erase Amanda's horrible memories and Jacqueline's worries, but at least he had two leads to pursue. And maybe a start toward setting things right.

"Have you found anything?"

Dillon started at the low whisper of Jacqueline's voice.

Pushing herself from the headboard, she sat straight in the bed. Her face was pale, her skin almost translucent. She looked unspeakably fragile, delicate, like a priceless porcelain doll.

He met her gaze. A grin touched the corners of his lips. "I found a connection."

Her eyes grew wide. She swung her legs over the side of the bed. "A connection? Between Swain and the newswoman Jancy Brock?"

"Between Swain and Dex Harrington." He allowed his face to break into a full-fledged grin. "Harrington prosecuted Swain's foster brother fifteen years ago for armed robbery. He had more witnesses and evidence than Carter has liver pills, but for some reason, Harrington let the guy off with probation."

"So Swain used some kind of influence with Harrington to help his foster brother?" Her eyebrows arched in a question, then puckered. "Swain doesn't strike me as the type who would help his own mother, let alone a foster brother."

"I suspect they were involved with one another in selling stolen goods. Nothing I can prove, unfortunately."

"So what exactly does this mean?"

"If Harrington was doing favors for Swain fifteen years ago, maybe he's doing the same now. Like giving him Mark's and Val's whereabouts."

She nodded, thinking it over. "Why? What's in it for Dex Harrington?"

"That's what I need to find out."

He knew she was expecting more, but it was the best he could do. For now. "If I can find out how Swain convinced Harrington to agree to the lenient sentence, maybe I can bring them both down. Provided Harrington is Swain's informant."

She stood and walked to the table. The scent of

her hair reached him before she did. Shampoo, crisp air and a sweet hint of vanilla.

He drew in a deep breath.

She sat down next to him. The dim light of the table lamp gleamed off the red tones in her hair, which shimmered in loose waves about her shoulders. Shadows cupped her high cheekbones. What he wouldn't give to be able to gather her in his arms, to kiss her again. He wouldn't pull back this time, not until both of them lost their senses.

He balled his fists under the table and reined in his imagination. Who was he trying to kid? Nothing had changed between them. Kissing Jacqueline was still a promise. A promise he couldn't make and couldn't keep.

But he wanted that kiss. And more. Much more. He wanted it so badly he ached.

She tilted her head, peering at him under furrowed brows. "What about Swain? Can you have him arrested?"

Dillon pulled his mind back to the matter at hand. He couldn't afford to let himself get distracted. He had to focus. Jacqueline's and Amanda's lives were at stake. "Amanda's identification of Swain's picture gives me enough evidence to get an arrest warrant for him. Britt Alcott is setting that in motion for me. By tomorrow, every police officer in the state will be looking for Buck Swain."

"So what do we do next?"

"We need to find out who Swain's mole is in the task force." He tore his gaze from her and looked down at the file folders strewn over the table. "We have two leads. Dex Harrington's case against

Swain's foster brother and the call that Amanda told us about. The one Mark got from Jancy Brock the night he was killed.''

"How do we go about following those leads?"

"The plea arrangement Harrington made with Swain's foster brother had to be agreed to by the district attorney. That would have been Bill Banks back then. He's a judge now. He'd be the one to talk to.''

She bit her bottom lip thoughtfully and nodded. "And Jancy Brock's call?"

"I pay Ms. Brock a visit. I'll go tomorrow morning.''

"What happened to *we?* I'm not just going to sit around and do nothing.''

Dillon reached across the table and rested his hand on hers. Her skin was soft under his touch, soft and delicate and vulnerable. "You and Amanda need to stay here. Judge Banks's chambers are just three floors down from the district attorney's offices. And that means the task force offices, as well. No use walking into the snake pit if we can avoid it.''

She said nothing, but he could see her acceptance in the tilt of her lips.

"I'll leave the Defender with you. I picked up more ammunition for it last night.'' He wished he could do more to reassure her. More to alleviate her worries.

Her gaze dropped to his open briefcase and locked on the silver barrel of the gun inside. She shuddered slightly. Setting her chin, she returned her gaze to Dillon's. Beneath the worry, a spark of determination and strength glowed in her eyes. "All right. Just don't take too long."

"I'M SORRY, REESE. I just can't remember back that far. A lot of water under the bridge since then." Judge Bill Banks leaned back in his leather chair, his Buddha-like paunch sticking out in front of him like a beach ball.

Dillon suppressed a groan. He'd been afraid of this. Bill Banks had a good memory, but fifteen years was a long time to recall a ordinary plea bargain. Especially with the number of cases the judge had dealt with since. His only alternative was to search for the written record, a search that could take a while. And the record wasn't likely to give him the information he needed, anyway. Dillon stood and thrust out his hand. "Thanks, Bill. I knew it was a long shot."

Banks stood and gave Dillon's hand a firm shake. "I don't suppose you would want to share the reason you're asking about a fifteen-year-old plea agreement." He narrowed his eyes. "I hope it doesn't have anything to do with politics."

Dillon gave him a disarming smile. "Hell, Judge, you know me better than that. Politics are about as valuable to me as a pail of hot spit."

Banks smiled, his twinkling eyes almost getting lost in the folds of his cheeks. "You're right. I do know you better than that. I don't know a less political man than you. Guess I was getting you confused with your boss. Speaking of your boss, you could ask Fitz about that fifteen-year-old plea agreement of yours. He was around back then and has a memory like the proverbial elephant. Besides, he was probably sniping over Harrington's shoulder. There's a long history of bad blood between those two.''

Dillon thanked the judge and left his chambers. Fitz. Why hadn't he thought of Fitz before? Not only might Fitz be able to help with his recollections of the armed robbery case, he would be more than eager to throw his weight behind ferreting out Swain's informant. If someone in his office was dirty, Fitz would want to cut out the dry rot as soon as possible. Dillon took the elevator up to the fifth floor and walked down the hall to the D.A.'s offices.

He strode past the reception desk and into the maze of hallways. It was a damn good thing Jacqueline and Amanda hadn't come with him. Talk about walking into the snake's pit.

He passed the closed doors of Dex Harrington's and Kit Ashner's offices. The hum of voices rose from behind both doors. They must be busy. Good. He'd rather not see either one this morning. He didn't know if he could keep his hands off their necks, and it would probably be a good idea to find out if they were guilty of any wrongdoing before strangling them.

Rounding the corner to Fitz's office, he almost ran headfirst into Detective Dale Kearney.

Kearney snapped to attention. ''Reese, I've been looking for you.''

Dillon regarded Kearney with a skeptical eye. He'd known a lot of ex-military men in his life, but none had absorbed the military aura like Kearney. The man's sharp movements and ''*sir, yes sir*'' intensity always made Dillon slightly uncomfortable. "What's up, Kearney?"

The detective lowered his voice in a conspiratorial tone. "I need to speak to you about Valerie Wallace."

Val. The bartender who was shot by Swain. Dillon's stomach tightened. "I heard you were with her when Swain took her out."

Kearney's gaze dropped to the floor. "I feel bad about that. Real bad. And that's the reason I needed to talk to you." His bright green eyes flicked up and down the empty hall. "Nobody knew I was bringing her to that apartment, Reese. Nobody outside the task force."

Dillon tensed. "I know."

"You think it was someone inside who leaked the location of the safe house to Swain?"

He studied the detective. Was Kearney merely trying to excuse himself for his blunder? Or could he be the informant trying to direct Dillon's suspicion elsewhere? "What do you think?"

A cloud passed over Kearney's face. If possible, his posture seemed to grow even more rigid. "It would explain a lot."

"Yes, it would."

The detective nodded. "I hear you've hidden the Schettler girl someplace."

Dillon's gut clenched. Warning bells clanged in his head, louder than a damned tornado siren. "That's right."

Kearney paused. His desire to ask about Amanda's location hung unsaid in the air like a foul smell. Apparently deciding the question would go unanswered, he gave his shoulders a crisp shrug. "Well, if you need anything, anything at all, just let me know."

Dillon flashed Kearney a phony smile and directed his gaze over the red-haired detective's head, dismissing him. "I'll do that." Like hell he would. He made a mental note to recheck Dale Kearney's files when he got back to the motel room. Kearney and Swain had been in the military at roughly the same time. If they had so much as set foot in the same commissary in the same week, Dillon wanted to know about it.

Breaking away, Dillon stepped into Fitz's office and closed the door behind him.

Fitz's silver head bowed over the papers on his desk, his hair catching the greenish glow of the fluorescent light overhead. He looked up. Lines tightened around his eyes and mouth. His movie-star visage seemed drained, tired. Very unlike Fitz. "What do you want, Reese?"

Dillon strode into the room and stopped in front of his desk. "What's wrong?"

A grimace twisted Fitz's lips. "You didn't watch the ten-o'clock news Saturday night, did you?"

No, he hadn't. Saturday night he'd been too busy running from a killer. "What did I miss?"

"An interview with Harrington. He announced he's running against me for district attorney in the fall. Word is he already has the governor and the Madison mayor in his camp."

So that was what had Fitz so worried. Politics. The only thing Fitz cared about more than justice. Dillon should have guessed. "Well, I may have an answer to your problem."

Fitz crooked an eyebrow. "Shoot."

"First I need to know what you remember about a case from fifteen years ago. A plea agreement."

"A fifteen-year-old case? I don't have a photographic memory, Dillon. You can look up the file as well as I can."

"I've already seen the file. I need more. It was Harrington's case. An armed robbery case against a Jim Plorman."

Fitz narrowed his eyes at the mention of Harrington's name. Dillon could almost see the political wheels turning. "Plorman?" He gave his head a shake, his eyes still glued to the papers on his desk. "I'm drawing a blank."

"It's the name of one of the foster families that took Buck Swain in. Jim Plorman is Swain's foster brother."

Fitz's gaze sharpened to a point. "Have you found something more about Swain?"

This was exactly the response he expected from Fitz. The district attorney had worked almost as hard as Dillon had to put Swain behind bars. And he'd done it in the glare of the political spotlight. When Mark and then Val had been murdered, that spotlight had grown mighty hot. "Just a hunch. Do you remember a case against Jim Plorman?"

He stroked his clean-shaven chin. "Vaguely. Harrington played his cases pretty close to the vest back then." A bitter smile curled the corners of his lips. "Still does."

"Did he cut a lot of one-sided deals?"

Fitz crooked a brow. "Why? Did he give away the farm on that one?"

"You could say that."

Fitz shook his head and heaved an exasperated sigh. "Doesn't surprise me. He never had a reputation for being tough on crime back then. Not that anyone will remember that when they see his name on the ballot. What does an old case of Harrington's have to do with Buck Swain?"

Dillon sank into a chair in front of Fitz's desk. His boss might not be able to remember much about the Plorman case, but he sure as hell would be a powerful ally in his search for Swain's mole in the task force. And he could use an ally about now. "I think someone in the task force is leaking information."

As the words sank in, a dark cloud passed over Fitz's features. His movie-star mouth tensed. "Media leaks?"

Dillon shook his head. "Whoever it is isn't leaking information to the media."

Fitz's brows tilted low over his eyes.

"He or she is leaking information to Swain."

Fitz's eyes bored into Dillon. "And because of this Plorman case, you think that person might be Dex Harrington."

Dillon nodded. "We need to find out."

A thousand-watt smile spread over Fitz's lips. His eyes crackled with intensity. The thought of Harrington in prison for helping Swain was making Fitz drool like a hungry dog. "What do you have on him? Any hard evidence?"

Dillon frowned. He didn't have a shred of evidence, hard or otherwise. "I wouldn't be fishing around for information on a fifteen-year-old case if I did."

Fitz nodded, unfazed. "I'll get someone on it right away. Someone from the outside with no ties to Harrington or the task force." He leaned back in his chair and pressed his steepled fingers against his lips, his brow furrowed in thought. "How about the little girl? Have you questioned her?"

"Yes."

"And?"

"Her testimony against Swain is pretty damning. It gives me enough for an arrest warrant."

Fitz nodded, all business, the dedicated and crafty prosecutor. "Have you gotten that child psychologist in to talk to her?"

"No."

His eyebrows shot up. "Well, what the hell are you waiting for? Where is she?"

Dillon's shoulders tensed. "I can't tell you."

"What?" Fitz narrowed his eyes. Although his voice was checked, the man seemed angry enough to eat the devil himself, horns and all. "Are you afraid I'm going to tell Harrington where he can find her?"

"I'll let you know as soon as—"

"As soon as what? What are you waiting for, Dillon? If this girl is a witness, I want to see her. Yesterday. And I want her under armed guard. What are you thinking?"

"She's safe where she is. And I intend to keep her that way."

"How? By not moving ahead with the case against Swain? By waiting until she has forgotten all the details of what she saw? By waiting until Harrington uses the negative publicity I'm getting on this case to put himself behind this desk? Is that what you're after?''

Dillon didn't say anything. He didn't want any of those things to happen, and Fitz knew it. But that still didn't mean Dillon was willing to risk bringing Amanda into the system.

''If you don't put the girl in protective custody, I can swear out a material witness warrant for her, Dillon.''

''That will solve your publicity problem, Fitz. Bullying a little kid.''

''I'll get the warrant issued for her mother.''

Anxiety stabbed Dillon like the chilled point of an ice pick. A material witness warrant would have half the cops in the county looking for Jacqueline. And when they found her, she and Amanda would be put in protective custody. Like Mark. Like Val.

He couldn't let it happen. ''I'm not bringing them in, Fitz.''

Fitz shook his head. ''You know damn well if anything goes wrong, I'll be the one held responsible.''

Dillon straightened to his full height. Fitz was wrong. *Dillon* would be the one responsible. *He* was the one who had given Jacqueline his word that he'd protect her daughter. And *he* was the one who wouldn't be able to live with himself if anything happened to that precious little girl. ''Sorry, Fitz. No one knows where the girl is until we find the snake who's leaking information to Swain. I'm not putting her life in danger.''

''And playing this game of yours isn't putting her life in danger?''

Dillon refused to rise to the bait.

A look of real regret washed over Fitz's chiseled features. "If you don't do this my way, Reese, you give me no choice."

Dillon held up a hand. The last thing he needed was the police breathing down his neck. He had enough trouble keeping Swain off their heels. "I need time, Fitz. Give me time to find out who's leaking information to Swain. Give your investigator from outside the task force time. I'll bring Amanda Schettler in as soon as we're sure who we're protecting her from."

Fitz leaned back in his chair and scrutinized Dillon through narrowed eyes. "I must be crazy for doing this, Dillon, but I'll give you forty-eight hours. After that, if my man doesn't come up with anything, the entire police force and sheriff's office will be looking for Jacqueline and Amanda Schettler. Have I made myself clear?"

Dillon turned and strode to the door. "Perfectly."

"And Dillon?" Fitz's voice rose from behind him. "You'd better pray nothing happens to that little girl in the meantime."

JACQUELINE PACED ACROSS the cramped motel room like a tiger in a cage. She glanced at her watch for the fifteenth time in fifteen minutes. A quarter after ten. Questions spun in her mind. Had Dillon been able to get a meeting with the judge? Had he learned anything?

She looked down at the motel-room phone. This waiting was killing her. If only he could call her, tell her what was going on. But he couldn't call. He couldn't take the chance that a phone call might be traced to this motel. To this room.

She glanced at her daughter. Amanda lay curled beneath the sheets, still sound asleep. She had slept more peacefully last night than she had since Mark had been killed. No screams in the middle of the night. No nightmares.

Jacqueline had been so afraid that forcing Amanda to remember her father's murder, forcing her to talk about it, would make her nightmares worse. So afraid Amanda would draw further into herself until Jacqueline could no longer reach her at all.

But just the opposite seemed to have happened. At least for one night, Amanda had been at peace. She had slept.

And once again it seemed Jacqueline had Dillon to thank.

"Mommy?" Amanda blinked up at her, pupils wide in the darkened room.

"Good morning, punkin."

Amanda stretched and offered her a little smile. "Can I have doughnuts for breakfast?"

"Doughnuts? Mr. Reese brought us some cereal. You like cereal."

"But I want doughnuts."

"Why doughnuts?"

"Because they're special. I want something special."

Jacqueline smiled at her daughter. This was the first time she'd been hungry since they'd left Dillon's house. Jacqueline wished she didn't have to deny her the doughnuts. She picked up the box of cartoon-inspired cereal Dillon had purchased this morning. If the unnatural neon colors and high sugar content didn't qualify as special, she didn't know what did. "This stuff is pretty special. We never have this at home."

At the sight of the zany box, Amanda's eyes lit up. She sat up and threw the blankets back. "Can I have some without milk?"

"If you brush your teeth and get dressed, you can have it whatever way you want."

"All right." She climbed out of bed and scurried into the bathroom.

While making the bed and straightening the room, Jacqueline allowed her thoughts to turn to Dillon. His consideration for Amanda, from his choice in cereal to his gentle manner when questioning her about Mark's death, warmed Jacqueline's heart. Mark had never gone grocery shopping, let alone selecting a cereal just for Amanda. He'd been too absorbed in the pub, both the business aspect of it and, most of all, the social aspect. He'd spent night after night at the pub far past working hours quaffing pint after pint with his friends. If he hadn't been so good at business, his partying would no doubt have drained the pub's profits years ago. Amanda had deserved a much better father than Mark.

And Jacqueline had deserved a much better husband.

A man like Dillon Reese.

She pushed the thought away and dedicated her attention to tucking the spread just so under the pillows. She couldn't let her mind wander to ridiculous fantasies. She had to focus on protecting Amanda from Swain. And protecting Amanda's heart and her own from wanting what could never be.

The gravel outside the motel room cracked and popped under the tires of an approaching car.

Jacqueline's nerves pulled taut. Was Dillon back already? She walked to the window and carefully pulled back a corner of the thick draperies. A sliver of sunlight pierced the gloom. She peered out.

A car was approaching the motel, all right, but it wasn't Dillon's rental car. It was a marked police car. It drove past their room and headed in the direction of the hotel office.

Anxiety prickled over her skin. Why were the police here? Could it have anything to do with Amanda? Or was their visit to the motel purely coincidental?

After all that had happened in the past few days, she didn't believe in coincidences. She laced up her boots and donned her parka. The motel office was only a few doors down. She could sneak to the corner of the building and see if she could overhear the officers' conversation with the motel manager. The whole trip would take a couple of minutes. If the cops' visit to the motel had nothing to do with Amanda, she and her daughter could be back in the room's safety before cereal grew mushy in milk. If it did, they would be in a better position to slip away unseen.

Her gaze rested on the silver barrel of Dillon's gun. She'd take the gun. Just in case. If the motel manager led the officers to the room, she would be better served to have the gun with her, rather than in the room waiting for them to find it.

She slipped the gun into her pocket and turned just as her daughter emerged from the bathroom. "Hey, punkin, I think I remember a vending machine next to the motel office. Let's see what they have. Maybe you can have doughnuts *and* cereal for breakfast."

"Cool," Amanda breathed. She quickly pulled on her coat and followed Jacqueline to the door. "Can Dorsey come with us? He doesn't want to be alone. He gets too scared."

Jacqueline smiled gently. "Of course Dorsey can come."

Amanda nodded and snatched the stuffed horse from the bed. They walked outside.

The motel was made up of three separate buildings surrounding the parking lot like a horseshoe. The office was on one of the ends of the horseshoe. It didn't take them long to find the vending machine around the corner from the office.

Jacqueline withdrew some quarters from her pocket as Amanda decided between apple and blueberry fruit pies.

The sound of voices drifted to her from around the corner. Her pulse picked up a beat. Tension inched up her spine. She peeked around the corner of the building. Two officers in blue uniforms stood at the sliding window that acted like a front desk. Thankfully their backs were to her.

One of the officers rapped on the glass. The man inside slid it open. A wave of cigarette smoke escaped into the outside air. "What can I do you for, Officers?"

Their voices were muffled, but she could still hear

them over the noise of the highway traffic. Jacqueline leaned closer to the corner of the building.

"Have you seen this woman around the motel?"

The gruff, chain-smoking man at the window chuckled. "She sure is a looker. I wish I'd seen her around here. Why? What did she do?"

"She has a little girl with her. About seven years old."

Jacqueline's breath caught in her throat. She closed her hand around the quarters, the coins digging into her flesh. It was no coincidence. The police were looking for her and Amanda.

But why?

Could Dillon have sent the police to pick them up? Had he found Swain's mole and sent a couple of officers to take her and Amanda to safety? No. He would have come to tell Jacqueline the good news himself. He never would have scared her like this.

Unless something had happened to him.

Fear niggled at the back of her neck. Could Dillon have been hurt? Could he have told the officers to pick them up because he couldn't do it himself?

No. He would have given them the room number. If the officers knew which room they were in, they wouldn't be at the office window showing pictures.

The task force. Jacqueline's heart pounded. Swain's informant could have sent the police to look for them. Her hands started to tremble. That was the most likely scenario. And the most frightening.

If Swain's mole was behind the police's visit, she and Amanda had to get out of here. Now.

Chapter Twelve

Dillon looked around the cavernous white room with warehouse-high ceilings. Big cameras and stands of lights scattered the studio, their cords taped to the floor. On one side of the room a desk perched on top of a short riser, the television station's call letters looming large on the backdrop behind it. The set of the local news.

Jancy Brock stood near the desk, examining her makeup in a hand-held mirror before her stint on the noon show. He'd seen her only a handful of times, but it always surprised him how petite she was. Much smaller than she appeared on television. Yet not fragile. There was a scrappy quality to her. And he knew from personal experience that once she got her teeth into a story, she dug in like a Jack Russell terrier.

Dillon strode toward her, his boots echoing on the waxed floor.

Looking up, she crooked a perfectly shaped eyebrow. A cagey smile spread over her lips. "Dillon Reese. I can honestly say you're the last person I expected to see walking into the studio. What's up?

Are you one of the wagons Fitzroy is circling after my big interview with Harrington on Saturday?''

''Fitz didn't send me.'' Fact was, Fitz would be none too happy if he knew Dillon was here. Where the media was concerned, Fitz believed in treading lightly.

''Really? Then what brings you to my neck of the woods? Do you have a hot scoop for me? Something I can use to write my ticket to a larger market?'' Her eyes fairly twinkled with curiosity.

''No, ma'am. But you have a scoop for me.''

''Me?'' An eager smile blossomed over her face. ''What could I possibly know that you don't?''

He didn't waste a beat. ''Did you call Mark Schettler the night he was killed?''

Jancy's eyes moved over his face, studying, assessing. She crossed her arms over her chest. ''Why? Am I in trouble?''

''That depends. Did you call him that night?''

''Yes, I did. I wanted to interview him.''

''How did you get his phone number?''

''He was at home.''

''Yes, but his phone number had been changed. Who gave it to you?''

She shrugged. ''He gave it to me. The man liked to see his face on TV. A lot of people are like that. I didn't dig out his phone number by any illicit means, if that's what you're implying.''

''And you called him from a pay phone on State Street?''

She thought for a moment. ''I was doing a story about college binge drinking at the fraternities, and

I hopped over to State Street to use a telephone. So? What's the point to all this?''

"When you called Mark, did you arrange to meet him later that night?"

"Hold on a second here, Counselor." She propped her fists on her hips. Her eyes narrowed, and she cocked her head to the side. Apparently Jancy Brock had answered all the questions she planned to. "Have you checked the constitution lately? I can meet with whomever I want."

"Did whomever you want include Mark Schettler on the night he was murdered?"

"If I answer that, what do I get in return?"

Now it was Dillon's turn to stand his ground. He gave her an I-mean-business stare. "I'm not here to make deals. Did you meet with Schettler the night he was murdered?"

"No." She smiled at him, a mischievous twinkle in her eye. "But I tried."

"What happened?"

"Your office nixed the idea. Really, that boss of yours loves us media types when we can be of use to him. But the moment he's sitting on top of a pow-der-keg case, he won't allow any media coverage. Zip."

And in this case, like most others in the past, Dil-lon agreed with him. "Maybe that's because he's interested in justice."

She shrugged. "I suppose. Me? I have no use for justice. Injustice makes for a better story."

Dillon ignored the comment. He was here to get answers, not to discuss ethics with Jancy Brock. "So Fitz called off your meeting with Mark Schettler?"

"I didn't say that."

"Who called off the meeting?" If she didn't give him a straight answer this time, he might just strangle her.

"My sister, actually."

Dillon arched his eyebrows in surprise. "Your sister? Who's your sister?"

"Kit Ashner."

Kit? Dillon's heart picked up a beat.

"My sister is one of those justice-loving types. You know, like you and your boss." Jancy shook her head as if loving justice were a sin. "She found out about the meeting somehow and nixed it."

Dillon clenched his fists at his sides. Kit had called off the meeting. At least with Jancy. But Mark had gone to the pub anyway. Had he gone for his own reasons, or because Kit never called *him* to cancel the meeting?

AFTER HE LEFT the television station Dillon had planned to go directly to Mylinski's house to see if he could catch the detective at home, but something—a nagging itch at the back of his neck, the tinge of a headache behind his eyes—had prompted him to go to the motel to check on Jacqueline and Amanda first.

He pulled his rental car in to the small parking lot behind the motel and climbed out. The constant hum of cars speeding by on the beltline highway was the only sound disturbing the still, brittle air. But Dillon could swear something was different about the motel.

Something was…disturbed.

He swept the parking lot and shabby, one-story

motel with his gaze. A handful of cars, mostly rusted-out buckets of junk, scattered the small lot. The drapes in all the rooms were drawn. Everything looked exactly the same as when he'd left this morning.

The hair on the back of his neck rose like the fur of a cat smelling danger. Something had changed. He could *feel* it. He pulled the motel key from his pocket and started for the room. The chill creeping up his back might just be paranoia, but he'd be damned if he'd ignore it. Paranoia might be the only thing standing between Jacqueline and Amanda and death.

He had to get them out of here.

Automatically he sank his hand into the pocket of his duster. His fingers touched nothing but lining. Damn. He'd left the Defender with Jacqueline. But if she had the gun, surely she'd be okay. She had to be.

He reached the weather-beaten door of room twenty-eight and slipped the key into the lock. The lock mechanism ground roughly. He pushed the door open and stepped inside.

The rumpled bed and an unopened box of breakfast cereal stared back at him. Jacqueline and Amanda were nowhere to be seen.

Alarm washed over Dillon in a wave the size of Texas.

He strode across the room. The bathroom door stood open. The interior was just as deserted as the rest of the room. They were gone.

Swain couldn't have found them. If he had, he would have shot them where they stood. Dillon clenched his fists and gritted his teeth against the image that flitted across his mind.

No. Swain hadn't found them. There must be another explanation.

The sense of foreboding clenching his stomach didn't let up. The explanations he came up with ranged from bad to horrible. He turned away from the empty bathroom and headed back out into the sunshine. He'd ask at the motel office. Maybe they would know something. Anything.

"Dillon."

He stopped dead in his tracks and spun in the direction of the whisper.

"Next to the car."

He followed the direction of the voice. Jacqueline's head peeked out from behind his rental car, her face white as the snow on the hillside behind her. The hood of a purple parka bobbed next to her, barely visible above the car.

Relief just about knocked him over. They were safe.

Raking the parking lot with his gaze, he ran back to the car. Without a word he unlocked the doors and they clambered inside, hunching down in the back seat the way they had the night he'd brought them to his house.

He lowered himself into the driver's seat, started the car and drove out of the parking lot and into the flow of traffic. "What the blazes is happening? Why did you leave the room?"

Jacqueline's pale face glowed in his rearview mirror. She swallowed hard and glanced at her daughter. "The police. I overheard two officers asking the man at the motel office if he'd seen a woman and a little girl. At first I thought something had happened to you. But—'' Her voice faltered. She drew a deep breath and coughed. ''They went from room to room. I—I didn't know if we could trust them.''

''Damn.'' He gripped the steering wheel. Fitz had promised to wait. He'd promised to give Dillon two days before he issued the material witness warrant. He'd said he would assign someone from outside the task force to investigate. Why would he suddenly change his mind?

Had he received pressure from the media? From Dex Harrington's campaign? Possibly. Whatever the reason Fitz had gone back on his word, it was clear that Dillon couldn't trust him to put this case above politics. Dillon was on his own.

''Why are the police looking for us?''

He looked back into the mirror. ''Apparently there's a material witness warrant out for you.''

Jacqueline peered questioningly at him, her eyes sunken, haunted. ''A material witness warrant? Like an arrest warrant?''

''Kind of. It's a warrant that directs the police to bring you into custody as an important witness. It's used for uncooperative witnesses.''

''But we're cooperating. Don't they know we're with you?''

He filled her in on his meeting with Fitz.

By the time he'd finished, her eyes were round with alarm. ''So now we're running from Swain *and* the police?''

Her question echoed to the very marrow of his bones. He'd never been on the other side of the law in his entire life. But unlike most first-time criminals, he knew the immense power and resources he faced.

The fear on Jacqueline's beautiful face told him that she, too, understood what they were up against. "So what do we do next?"

It was a damned good question. And he'd better come up with a damned good answer.

He clenched the steering wheel and stared ahead at the light traffic on the highway. There was one place he could go where neither Swain nor the police would think to look for them. At least, not right away. A place they would be safe while he figured out what to do next.

He raised his eyes to the rearview mirror and offered Jacqueline and Amanda his best attempt at a confident smile. "How do you feel about taking a little fishing vacation?"

JACQUELINE HUDDLED in the back seat of the rental car and tried to sort through the names and questions jumbled in her mind. Kit Ashner. Dex Harrington. Jancy Brock. Buck Swain. Who was in league with whom? Who could they trust? And how could they prove the guilty parties were indeed guilty? The questions kept coming, pounding relentlessly like a stiff, cold rain. She hugged Amanda closer. So much had happened in the past few days, but here she was back where she started. Afraid of the police. Distrusting the system. On the run.

Except one thing was different. One thing had changed since the night she'd smuggled Amanda from the pub. She'd been alone then. Utterly alone with the entire weight of Amanda's survival on her shoulders.

Dillon was with her now. And if anyone could keep them safe, he could.

She looked at his strong shoulders. The dark hair curling around the collar of his black duster. She thought of the determination in his eyes. The tenderness in his voice. The passion in his kiss.

And now he was risking his career to protect them.

She swallowed into a parched throat and pulled herself out of her thoughts in time to feel the car jar over potholes and sink into mud. They traveled at least a mile down the winding dirt road. Finally they came to a stop.

"We're here." Dillon's smoky drawl reached into the back seat. He swung out of the car and opened the rear door.

Cool afternoon air wafted into the vehicle, fanning Jacqueline's cheeks. Crisp. Refreshing. Amanda climbed off Jacqueline's lap and out the open door. Jacqueline followed.

She blinked back the brilliant afternoon sun and looked around. They seemed to be firmly planted in the middle of nowhere, nothing but the naked branches of trees and brush to witness their arrival. Her eyes were drawn immediately to the curving bed of the Wisconsin River. Chunks of ice floated past in the powerful current. Scrub brush dotted the bank. Each naked, twisted branch glistened with ice, multifaceted as fine-cut diamonds. The air smelled wet and fresh with the late-winter thaw.

Jacqueline filled her lungs with the sweet fragrance and raised her arms over her head, attempting to stretch the tension from the muscles in her back. "It's beautiful."

Dillon strode up and stopped next to her. His masculine scent stirred the calm air and urged her pulse into a faster tempo. "It's Mylinski's cabin. He brought me here about a year ago. Forced me to stay for two days and fish. Didn't catch a thing, but I sure did a heap of relaxing."

She looked at him skeptically. She'd seen for herself how driven he was, how he lived and breathed his work. It was evident in everything from the intensity of his eyes to the decor of his home. "You? Relax? Yeah, right."

He gave her a caught-me-in-a-lie smile that sizzled along her nerves. "You got me. This place drove me crazier than popcorn on a hot skillet. Nothing to do but watch the river current and pace. Mylinski finally agreed to drive me back to civilization because he was afraid I'd wear a path in his green vinyl floor." He shook his head at the memory. "But I can see how it might relax other people. Normal people."

A chuckle rose effortlessly from her lips.

"Was that a laugh I heard?" Dillon smiled. "See? You're relaxing already. Mylinski swears the place has magical powers." The smile faded from his lips, and he looked down at her, his eyes filled with a softness she hadn't seen before. "You'll be safe here. At least for a little while."

Safe. She drank in the word like a woman dying of thirst. After the scare she and Amanda had had with the police this morning, it had felt as if they would never be safe again. They had hidden in the alley. No car. No money. Nowhere to go. Until Dillon had shown up. Until he'd brought them here.

"Mommy, look at this little house."

She turned in the direction of Amanda's excited voice.

Her little girl stood outside a building about the size of a linen closet. "Can I go in here? Can this be my fort?"

Jacqueline stifled a smile. At least this river refuge had fired Amanda's imagination, and that was enough magic to have Jacqueline believing in anything Mylinski could dream up. "Sorry, punkin, but that's the bathroom."

Amanda looked at her as if she'd lost her mind. "The bathroom?"

"It's called an outhouse." Dillon unlatched the door and pulled it open. "The cabin has running water in the kitchen, but there's no bathroom. This is what you city folks call 'roughing it.'"

Amanda planted her boots at the entrance and, leaning forward, peered inside. She looked back to Jacqueline and screwed up her face. "It's a bench with a hole in it, Mommy."

Dillon's chuckle tickled the air. "That's right. It's a bench with a hole. And I'm going to toss you right in." He swooped Amanda up in his arms and kissed her cheek.

The sweet sound of her little girl's squeal and giggle brought tears to Jacqueline's eyes. She'd been so afraid she'd never hear that carefree laugh again. So afraid she'd never again see her sunny, imaginative daughter.

And once again, she had Dillon to thank.

How did he know just what to do, what to say to draw Amanda out of her fear? As far as Jacqueline knew, he'd never had children of his own. Yet he seemed to know instinctively just the right amount of teasing, just the right touch of encouragement her little girl needed to emerge from her cocoon like a butterfly in summer.

Jacqueline drew a deep breath of fresh, wet air into her lungs and feasted on the music of Amanda's laughter. A contented smile stretched over her lips. An inner peace beckoned her. Dillon seemed to know exactly what *she* needed, as well.

Is this what he'd be like if he didn't have this crusade hanging over his head, controlling his life? A great father figure for Amanda? A tender and caring lover for her?

Her smile faded. The familiar worry replaced it, nipping at her heels. What would Amanda do without him when this was over?

And what would *she* do?

He set Amanda back on the ground and gave her a wink and a grin. "Let's check out the inside of the cabin. I'll race you."

Amanda took off in the direction of the cabin, her little legs churning through the snow as fast as they could go. Dillon dashed after her. Inhaling another breath of fresh, sweet air and blocking the worries from her mind, Jacqueline walked on behind.

Perched on stilts to keep the floodwaters at bay, the cabin huddled on the edge of the woods. It was small, a one-story affair with green-painted clapboard siding and louvered windows. Amanda scampered up the steps leading to the door. "I won, Mr. Reese. I won."

Dillon stopped at the bottom of the stairs and smiled up at her. "First of all, you need to call me Dillon. And secondly, you sure run faster than my old bones can carry me."

Amanda giggled again and yanked on the doorknob. It didn't budge. "It's locked, Mr. Ree— Dillon."

"Yes, it is. But..." Dillon reached under the cabin, feeling along the edge with his hand. He straightened and held a key in the air with a flourish. "For a cop, Al Mylinski is remarkably trusting."

He joined Amanda at the top of the stairs, unlocked the door and pushed it open. Amanda scampered inside. Judging from the patter of her footsteps audible in the still afternoon air, she was running from one room to another. Exploring, like a normal seven-year-old.

Like a normal seven-year-old. Jacqueline savored that thought, rolling it around in her mind like fine wine on the palate. Maybe someday everything *could* be normal again. She hadn't allowed herself to think of that possibility since the night their nightmare had begun.

Dillon held the door open and gazed down at her. "After you, ma'am." A look just short of a smile spread over his lips and crinkled the corners of his dark eyes. A look steeped in wanting. A look just for her.

A tremor scrambled along her nerves. Grabbing the handrail for support, she mounted the steps to the door. The doorway was narrow, and he didn't move when she wedged in next to him to enter. So close she could feel the heat of his body. So close she could smell his clean, masculine scent.

She wanted him to take her in his strong arms right there. Hold her and never let her go. She knew the way his body felt pressed against hers, the way his skin smelled, the way his lips tasted. And she wanted to experience those sensations again. And again. She wanted more than a single kiss. More than a single night.

And that was the problem. A single night was all Dillon could offer. He'd given his heart to his crusade long ago. And that was one thing even the magic in Mylinski's cabin couldn't change. Composing herself, she slid past him into the cabin.

Once inside, she tried to focus on the cabin's interior and not on the man next to her.

The cabin was larger inside than she'd anticipated—two good-sized bedrooms and a fairly big room that included the kitchen and living area.

In one corner a basketball-sized beehive, the bees long since dead, hung from the ceiling. In another, a bass swam across an oak plaque. She glanced around at the comfortable, rustic furniture. The warm kitchen. The thick rugs dotting the floor. This place felt cozy. A place to rest. A place to heal. A place to fill her soul.

Soaking in the music of Amanda's giggle and Dillon's only-for-her look, she could almost believe this place *was* magical. That it *could* change things.

She could almost believe they were safe.

THE PHONE RANG.

Buck Swain swore as he ran the brass brush

through the barrel of his weapon one more time. He knew what would be on the other end of the phone line. More orders. More complaints. And he didn't want to hear it.

He hadn't told his "partner" about his failure to take care of the girl and her mother when he'd chased them from Reese's house. He hadn't wanted to put up with the flak. His failure made him angry enough. He didn't need the coward's whining complaints heaped on top of it.

He gritted his teeth at the memory of them speeding away on that damned snowmobile. Reese and the woman would pay.

He set the rifle carefully on the table and threaded a patch of cloth through the eye of his rod. The phone kept ringing.

Damn. He might as well get this over. He picked up the receiver and cradled it in the crook of his neck. "Yeah?"

"Where the hell have you been?" the angry voice erupted.

Swain snarled and ran the patch through the barrel of his weapon. He'd had just about enough of this. If his association with the person on the other end of the line wasn't so profitable, he might consider adding a name to his list of things that had to be taken care of. "I hope you're calling to tell me where the girl is. Otherwise I don't want to hear it."

Silence on the other end.

The coward didn't know. Just as Swain had expected. "So if you don't know where she is, what do you want?"

"I'll find her. Soon," the smooth voice promised. "I got a little help from an unexpected source today."

"What source?"

He could almost hear the smile on the other end of the line. "Suffice it to say that every cop in the county is looking for her."

Swain twisted the cap closed on his bottle of solvent and rolled his eyes. "And how is that supposed to help us?"

"Can you pull off another shot like the one you took at Val Wallace, the bartender? Or was that just dumb luck?"

Swain looked at his weapon lying dismantled on the table. A few more minutes and it would be squared away. A thrill worked up his spine. The kind of thrill he always got when thinking about a difficult shot. He smiled and ran his fingers over the smooth, cold barrel of his weapon. The tougher the shot, the better.

He pushed out of his mind the fact that this shot would be aimed at a kid. A man had to do what he had to do. "There's no such thing as luck, dumb or otherwise. Not where my shooting is concerned. The girl is as good as dead."

"And the mother and Reese, too. I've had it with the lot of them."

Swain smiled. As if he needed this coward's permission. He'd planned to kill Reese all along. "Just tell me where and when."

Chapter Thirteen

Dillon leaned against the doorjamb and watched Jacqueline tuck the blankets securely around Amanda's little body and go through their bedtime ritual of back rubs and I-love-yous. He drank in the sound of Jacqueline's voice, studying the drape of her hair, the curve of her neck as she ran her hand over her little girl's back.

Taking a deep breath of the cabin's slightly musty air, he rolled his shoulders. The knot that had twisted when he'd walked into that motel room and found them gone had finally loosened a touch. But relaxation was still far from his reach.

Seeing Jacqueline in such an intimate setting, hearing her voice, smelling her sweet vanilla scent wound another kind of tension, nearly as painful, deep inside him. She was a beautiful woman, yes, but no beautiful woman had ever affected him this way before. She was more than merely a pretty face and a tempting body. Much more. She was a unique blend of strength and vulnerability, a wounded warrior, a fierce mother. One moment she looked as if she was on the edge of breaking down, the next she was driving a snowmobile into the line of fire to save his life.

And he'd never wanted any woman more.

His fingertips itched to touch her satin skin. His lips ached to kiss her long, graceful neck. But he couldn't have her. Not the way he wanted. Not the way she deserved.

He'd grown up in a small, close-knit family, and he'd always assumed he'd have a little brood of his own, a woman like Jacqueline wearing his ring and cuddled in his arms on cold winter nights.

But he'd given up those expectations, those dreams, ten years ago. He couldn't go back to them. No matter how much he wanted to. He should know that by now. He should accept it. He'd had ten long years to get used to the idea. Instead of a family, he had his work. Instead of love, he had the promise of justice.

But somehow, in the warmth of her presence, he wanted to forget everything. His loss, his pain, his whole damned "crusade," as Jacqueline called it. Everything but her.

He tore his gaze from her and forced his feet to carry him back to the living room to the files spread across the giant wooden spool Mylinski called a coffee table. He needed to focus on finding Swain's mole in the task force. He needed answers.

He lowered himself to the couch and stared at the paper spread across the spool. Tonight he'd tried once again to reach Mylinski. He'd called both his home and the precinct from a tavern downriver. Again, he'd had no luck. And in spite of all the reassurances he'd given Jacqueline about the detective's ability to take care of himself, he was beginning to worry.

He pushed the worry from his mind and picked up a file from the table. He'd already scoured every line, every word, but he would have to do it again. And again. Until he found something. Because they couldn't hide in this cabin forever. Sooner or later someone would find them. The police. Swain.

And he couldn't bear to think what could happen when their time ran out.

JACQUELINE LEANED FORWARD and kissed Amanda's cheek. Her little girl's eyelids fluttered at the touch, but her breathing stayed steady, low and deep. No stirring, no waking. No signs of a nightmare.

Jacqueline exhaled a grateful sigh and replayed in her mind the events since Dillon had whisked them away from the motel. The patter of Amanda's adventuring footsteps when she explored the cabin, her wide-eyed fascination with the dried beehive, the symphony of her giggle. A smile flitted across Jacqueline's lips. Her baby was coming back.

Thanks to Dillon.

It seemed so long ago that she'd cursed his name, blaming him for putting her little girl in danger. He'd done so much for Amanda, for her, since then. He'd kept his promises. He'd been willing to lay down his life to protect them. He'd shown Amanda kindness, understanding, tenderness and love to bring her back from the trauma of Mark's death and set her on the road to recovery. A blessing indeed. And more than enough to redeem him.

She'd felt him watching her tuck Amanda under

the covers, his gaze traveling over her like a warm
caress, his breath a whisper in the still night.

A deep ache seized her. An ache of loneliness. Of
emptiness. Of need. How would it feel to have Dillon's hands caressing her? To have his lips roaming
over her bare skin? To have him close to her, inside
her, filling her?

But could she stand to have those things only for
one night? Because that was all she would get. Dillon
was with her now, but as soon as he'd resolved the
case, he'd be gone. She knew this as surely as she
knew anything. He lived for justice, for avenging his
sister's death.

And she wanted more than that.

Her fantasy would have to remain just that, a fantasy. One she would keep locked away in a private
place in her heart.

She kissed Amanda's silken cheek, rose from the
bed and padded to the door. With one last glance at
her little girl, she closed the door and ventured out
into the living room.

He sat on the battered old brown couch, those intense black eyes focused on the papers spread out on
the giant wooden spool in front of him. Worry lined
his forehead and mouth. The muscles in his shoulders
and arms were visibly taut. He pored over the papers
as if through effort alone he could make the answers
he was looking for appear.

Her stocking feet silent on the vinyl floor, she
crossed the room and lowered herself onto the corner
of the worn cushions next to him. Her skin tingled,
coming alive with his closeness. ''Find anything
more?''

''Not yet.''

She sighed. It was the same exchange they'd had countless times. Heaviness settled in the pit of her stomach. ''Maybe we should face the obvious. Maybe there's nothing in those files to find.''

He raised his eyes from the paper. The bleak expression on his face told her he'd already considered the possibility. He shook his head stubbornly. ''Maybe there isn't. Maybe I'm wasting my time. But I can't give up trying.''

''You never give up, do you?'' She didn't know why she asked the question. After all, she knew the answer. Hearing him say the words wouldn't change anything.

He turned away from the papers, his attention riveted on her. ''I won't give up until Swain is behind bars and Amanda is safe.''

''And what happens then?''

''Amanda will testify at his trial. She'll have to, Jacqueline. I'm sorry.''

Her stomach clenched as the words left his lips. It wouldn't be easy, but Amanda would get through it. She would put Swain in prison for good. Where he couldn't hurt her. Where he couldn't hurt anyone ever again.

''And then what? What will happen to us?''

He pivoted toward her on the couch, his knees almost touching hers. The naked bulb of the lamp behind him cast a harsh glare over the planes of his face and cloaked his eyes in shadow. But even through the shadow, she could see a shimmer of regret in his eyes. ''You know what will happen.

Amanda will go back to school. You'll go back to brewing beer.''

"And you?"

"I'll go on to the next case."

She nodded. Of course she'd known what he would say. The very thing that made him shoulder the responsibility of protecting Amanda, that fueled his search for Swain and his accomplice, would propel him on to the next case—love for his sister, guilt over her death. But still, to have him state his intentions out loud made her feel hollow inside. "And you'll never give up until all the murderers in Wisconsin are behind bars, right?''

Dillon cocked his head at the resentful tone in her voice. An expression of concern passed over his face. Concern and regret. He studied her eyes, as if trying to read her thoughts. "I can't give up. You know that."

"Yes, I know." She pushed the image of his sister's bloody body from her imagination, the image she knew haunted Dillon every hour of every day. She should stand and walk out of the room, leave him to his guilt and pain. Protect her heart and her daughter's. But somehow she couldn't. Not yet. She had to give it her best shot. She couldn't tuck her feelings away without finding out once and for all whether they had even a whisper of a chance. She leaned forward and laid her fingers gently on one balled fist. "Janey's death wasn't your fault, Dillon. You couldn't have prevented her death."

His eyes grew dark, unreadable. A muscle worked along his jaw.

"I know you gave her the tuition money, and you

bought her the bus ticket. But you couldn't have known what would happen. No one could have known.''

His gaze dropped to her fingers. He stared as though studying every knuckle, every nail, but she knew he couldn't see anything through the despair clouding his vision. Silence stretched over the room, no sound but the faint ticking of a clock in the kitchen.

''Janey deserved to go to the college of her choice, Dillon. She wanted to go. And if she was anything like her big brother, she wouldn't have given up until she got what she wanted.''

He raised an eyebrow as if considering her statement. Finally he nodded, still staring at her fingers with unseeing eyes. ''There was no stopping her when she set her sights on something.''

''Even if you had known something bad was going to happen, you couldn't have stopped her.''

''No.''

''And would she have wanted you to focus your life on seeking justice? To the exclusion of everything else?''

''It's something I have to do.''

''To ease your guilt?''

He raised his eyes to hers, their black intensity sending a shiver through her that shook her bones. ''To make things right.''

The conviction in his eyes, in his voice drove into her heart like a cold steel blade. But she couldn't leave it at that. She still couldn't force herself to walk away. She had to push, she had to fight. For him.

And for her. "Your crusade won't bring Janey back."

"Don't you think I know that? Don't you think I have to face that every day?"

"Then what good is it all?"

"It's no good. None of it is any good." He covered her hand with his and let out a tortured breath. "I always thought I would have a family of my own. A wife, kids, a real home. But I can't do that now. Not with what happened to Janey. Not with her murderer still out there. Not with all the murderers still out there."

"Don't you think she'd want you to have those things? Don't you think that she would want you to be happy?"

"I'm sure she would. And maybe I will be someday. Maybe someday I can make a difference. Maybe someday I can set things right. But until then, I can't pretend that murders don't happen, that other families aren't losing the people they love. I can't just pretend. I have to do something."

"For Janey?"

He nodded. His shoulders seemed to droop with despair. "And for myself."

Sadness seeped into her, sadness and loss and regret so deep it penetrated her bones and seeped into her soul. "I wish..." She let her words trail off, not wanting to face the anguish in her heart, not wanting to put it out in the open. She tore her gaze from his and focused on her hands in her lap, joined with his.

He raised a hand to her face. Running his fingers gently along her jaw, he lifted her chin, compelling her to look at him. "What do you wish?"

"I wish your crusade wasn't so personal."

His brow furrowed.

Her heart thumped heavily in her chest. Her throat ached with emotion. Drawing in a deep breath, she pushed the words from her mouth. "I want you, Dillon. All of you. And while justice is the focus of your life, I can't have you."

Silence buzzed in her ears. Even the ticking of the clock seemed to have stopped. He remained still, frozen except for his eyes. Sadness hung in their depths like shadows. Shadows so thick, daylight could never dispel them.

Untangling her hands from his, she stood and forced her legs to carry her toward the short hall leading to the bedrooms.

"Jacqueline." His smoky drawl wrapped around her name with such intimacy, it stole her breath.

She stopped but didn't turn to look at him. Seeing the regret in his eyes would be too wrenching. Too painful.

"Just so you know, I wish, too."

She swallowed. She did know. But it didn't change anything. Nothing could.

DILLON STARED at the shadows of trees that reached through the windows and splayed across the bedroom's darkened ceiling. He'd been awake for hours, staring at the ceiling, reviewing Jacqueline's words in his mind. If only he could have told her that his crusade for justice wouldn't come between them. If only he could have taken her in his arms right then, kissed her and promised her the world.

Instead he lay in bed alone, watching the quarter

moon rise in the sky, straining to hear sounds of her rustling in the next bedroom, cursing himself, his crusade, his life. He couldn't give Jacqueline what she wanted. What she needed. What he needed, as well. The loss was too thick in his heart. The pain too acute. He couldn't change the past. And without changing the past, he couldn't change his future.

A noise in the hallway caught his attention. The soft padding of feet. The quiet whisper of breath. Her figure glided into his room, the soft curves of her body silhouetted against the moonlight and shadow stretching through the window. She clasped the front of his wrinkled white dress shirt closed with her hand, the buttons undone, the shirttail brushing the tops of her bare thighs. Her hair fell loose, draping her shoulders like a cloak.

His breath lodged in his throat. He watched, unable to move, unable to speak as she closed and locked the door and turned to face him.

Arousal pooled in his groin. Arousal only she could inspire, and only she could satisfy. He wanted to go to her, to wrap her in his arms, but he couldn't touch her. Not yet. He had to know why she was here. He had to hear the words. "Jacqueline?"

She licked her lips. Her eyes shimmered in the night. "I need your arms around me."

"I can't promise you anything. No future."

"I know. It doesn't matter. I can spend all night staring at the ceiling and wishing for what can never be, or I can grab whatever you can give with both hands." She opened the shirt and slid the starched fabric off her shoulders. The cotton skimmed over her legs as it dropped to the floor. The moonlight caressed the perfect round globes of her breasts, the flat expanse of her belly, the soft hair between her legs. "I need you, Dillon."

Flames of desire spread through him like unchecked wildfire. Want pulsed inside him like a life force. In one motion he threw the sheets back and stood. Then he was beside her. The cool air skimmed over his bare, heated skin. His need pressed against the cotton of his briefs. He reached out to touch her, to pull her to him, to wrap her in his embrace.

Her skin was as soft as he'd imagined. Butter soft. Doeskin soft. He pulled her tight against his body, cradling her head like a precious gift. Hungrily he claimed her lips with his own.

She leaned into him and wrapped her arms around his neck. Her fingers intertwined with his hair. She answered his need with her need, his want with her want. Her tongue tangled with his, danced with his, made love to his.

He couldn't get enough. He pulled her closer, tighter against him. Her full, soft breasts pushed against his bare chest, the sweet heat of her branding his flesh. He left her lips and trailed kisses down the satin column of her neck and over the delicate perfection of her collarbone. Her scent surrounded him, infused him. The clean, sweet fragrance of her flavored with the mellow tones of vanilla. He wanted to taste all of her. Feel all of her. Lose himself in her.

He lowered her to the rumpled sheets of the bed. Standing, he drank in the sight of her bare skin against dark sheets. His gaze lingered over her, taking in each curve, each shadow. She was everything from his fantasies and more. Much more. Hunger blasted through him, powerful, relentless.

Hooking his thumbs in the waistband of his briefs, he pushed them down, over the straining bulge of his desire and down his legs, until he was free and naked before her.

Fire lit her eyes. A secret smile graced her lips.

He lowered himself to the bed and stretched out next to her, skin against skin. Gathering her in his arms, he touched his mouth to the mounds of her breasts. Capturing her nipple, he licked and teased and tasted.

She moaned softly. Her fingers combed his scalp and tangled in his hair.

Having savored one breast, he moved to the other, the nipple instantly pebbling under the flick of his tongue. He'd waited so long for this. To touch her, to feel her, to taste her. Tonight she was his, and he was hers. And nothing, not the police, not Swain, not even the constant demands of justice could take this moment away from them.

He moved down the flat expanse of her belly, littering kisses all the way. He couldn't get enough. When he reached her most private place, her quiet moans washed over him like the breaking tide, sweeping him into ecstasy.

She arched into him. Her breathing crescendoed. He took her to the edge of the cliff, and then refused to let her go over, bringing her to the pinnacle again and again. He wanted to fill her need. He wanted to chase away the worry and fear that had haunted her eyes since he met her.

If only for one night.

Finally her release came, shuddering through her body in waves. He held her close, letting the delicious tremor of her body shake him.

Her body stilled. Her breathing slowed.

Need pulsing inside him, he slid beside her and looked into her eyes. He wanted to see her strength reflected in the blue pools as he entered her, filled her, loved her.

She returned his gaze, her eyes clear, blissful and still so eager. Placing her hands on his chest, she pressed him back against the bed. "Relax. It's my turn."

Relax. Easier said than done. Desire pounded through him. He gulped air.

She moved down his chest, his stomach, her lips wet and warm, her hair trailing over his skin in chestnut wisps that whipped his blood.

She moved down the trail of hair that bisected his stomach and over his surging need, her tongue flicking, feeding his passion.

He clenched his teeth. It took every shred of willpower to keep from tipping into oblivion. He clutched her shoulders in desperate hands. "Jacqueline. Please."

She moved up his body and straddled him, her warm wetness making his need so acute, so painful, he could barely keep from rolling her onto her back and driving into her.

Slowly she lowered herself over him and accepted him into her body. His breath escaped with a whoosh. He was inside her, joined to her in the way only lovers can join. Their bodies, their hearts, their souls melded together.

If only for this moment.

He circled her waist with his hands. She rose and fell over him, accepting the length of him deep inside her, the waves of passion building until he couldn't hold out any longer. He felt her crest just as he did, soaring, shattering, splintering. The need inside him pouring out.

And she accepted his need and matched it with her own.

Chapter Fourteen

If possible, Jacqueline was even more beautiful in the first rays of dawn. Dillon propped himself on an elbow in the bed beside her and watched the steady rise and fall of her breasts in the gentle light. Her eyelids fluttered and a soft smile skittered over her lips.

Dreaming. Dillon smiled. He didn't need to sleep in order to dream. His dream was right here in the circle of his arms.

He glanced at the ancient clock radio sitting on the bedside table and willed the hands to move more slowly. He didn't want this time to end. Didn't want to awake to another day of struggling for justice. He was tired of the criminal justice system, tired of his crusade, tired of putting criminals behind bars only to have them out on the streets in a few short years causing more innocent people pain.

He was bone tired, and he wanted to sleep. He wanted to dream forever.

Jacqueline moaned softly beside him and her eyelids fluttered open. She looked up at Dillon, a smile spreading over her lips, ripe with remembered loving. ''Good morning, cowboy.''

''Good morning.'' He lowered himself over her and kissed her, indulging in her taste, in the satin feel of her breasts pressed against his chest. How could he go back to a life without this? How could he never touch her, never kiss her, never bury himself inside her again?

He pulled back from the kiss and peered into her eyes. So clear, so blue, so blissfully peaceful. If only he could keep her this way. In his bed. Happy. Loved.

But he couldn't. Soon he would have to turn his mind to Swain, to material witness warrants—to protecting the innocent and making the guilty pay. Soon the feel of Jacqueline's skin would be only a sweet memory.

He lowered his head to the pillow beside hers, savoring the closeness for a few extra moments. ''I'll have to go into town today to call Mylinski again. For what good it will do. The tavern where I used the phone last night won't be open until noon.''

He tried not to notice the bleakness that settled over her features, the little lines of worry that creased the bridge of her nose, the weight of reality that settled back on her shoulders like a yoke.

A pain cramped the muscles in his neck and shoulders. He couldn't change reality. Not for her or for himself. He forced himself to continue. ''Other than that, there isn't much I can do right now. We'll just have to sit tight and—''

She held a finger to his lips, halting the flow of his words.

He kissed her finger. Inhaling deeply, he drew in her scent. A scent he would remember for the rest of his life.

She replaced her finger with her lips, kissing him firmly, hungrily. When she pulled back, the sadness in her eyes was almost unbearable. "Will you do something for me?"

"Anything I can, darlin'," he whispered, and he meant it. With every fiber of his being.

"Will you pretend?"

He looked at her in question.

"Will you pretend that we do have a future? Just for a couple of days? For as long as we're here at the cabin? You, me and Amanda. Can we all be happy, just for a little while?"

Dillon's throat tightened. Her request was so simple. So naked. How could he not comply? It was what he wanted, too, after all. What could a few days hurt? After that they would have a lifetime of regrets. She was offering him a shot at heaven. And he was going to take it.

"Yes, we can pretend. It'll be my pleasure." He pulled her close and kissed her. Let the devil take tomorrow. He had all he wanted, all he needed, right now.

"ARE YOU READY?"

Buck Swain clenched the phone in his injured hand. A smile spread over his lips. "You found them?"

"Almost. Reese made a call from a tavern along the Wisconsin River last night. One of the regulars at the bar confirmed that it was him. The area is being canvassed as we speak. Are you ready to move?''

Swain glanced at his weapon. It lay in its case on the kitchen table. Cleaned, polished. Not just combat ready, but inspection ready, as well. His smile grew. He wished Reese could appreciate the trouble he'd gone to to ensure this kill would be picture-perfect. Too bad the lying SOB would be dead long before he had the chance. ''I'm good to go. Just give me the location.''

''MOMMY, LOOK WHAT I FOUND.'' Amanda held a broad piece of bark in the air.

''Wow. That's a big piece, punkin.'' She glanced at Dillon standing next to her and gave him a little smile. She wanted to take his hand in hers, to soak up his warmth like a sponge, but they had decided to keep their relationship merely friendly in front of Amanda. There would be time for touching tonight after she'd tucked her little girl safely under the covers. Then they could explore each other, savor each other, love each other.

For what little time they had.

She directed her mind back to Amanda. The night would be wonderful, but she would cherish the day, too, exploring the river, playing with Amanda on its twisting sandbars. She would drink in the moments like a precious elixir, experiencing both the days and nights to their fullest. She knelt next to Amanda and studied the chunk of bark in her little hands more closely. ''What are you going to do with it?''

''I'm going to make a boat and float it down the river.''

Dillon crouched, joining them on the moist sand. "That's one great idea."

"First I have to get a guy to put in the boat."

Dillon crooked an eyebrow. "A guy?"

Amanda nodded emphatically. "Like a person or animal."

He eyed the hunk of bark. "I hate to say it, but I don't think a person or animal is going to fit in a boat that small."

Amanda rolled her eyes at Jacqueline and let out an exasperated sigh. "Not a *real* person or animal, silly. A *guy*."

Dillon nodded, duly corrected.

Jacqueline stifled a laugh. Amanda had always had her own little imaginary world and her own vocabulary to go along with it.

She glanced at Dillon. He looked so intent and serious. He might not know Amanda's favorite terms, but he was willing to learn. A warm glow flowed down her spine and spread outward in waves, washing over her from head to toe.

Dillon held up a hand. "Now let me see if I've got this straight. A guy is pretend."

"No." Amanda propped a little fist on one hip, her voice taking on the instructional quality of a patient, if bossy, teacher. "A guy is just little. Like a little plastic elephant. Or one of my dollhouse people. Or something you make. I'm going to make a guy for this boat."

He nodded in understanding. "And what are you going to use to make your guy?"

She raised her little shoulders in a shrug. "Don't know yet." She eyed the flat expanse of the sandbar, zeroing in on a tangle of scrub brush directly across the narrow river channel from the cabin. "Maybe sticks."

He stroked his chin in a thoughtful manner. "Sticks. Good idea."

Amanda gave him a serious look. "Yes, I thought so." With a brief nod, she scampered off in search of guy-making materials, cradling the hunk of bark in one arm like a baby doll. The hood of her parka flopped up and down on her back as she ran.

Jacqueline watched her go, a glow of gratitude filling her chest. Amanda had come so far in the past few days. This morning she'd even been brave enough to separate herself from Dorsey the Horsey. She'd decided to leave him home in the cabin for fear he'd get wet and sandy if he came on their adventure. She was bouncing back to her old self, right in front of Jacqueline's eyes. Given time, Amanda might recover from what she'd witnessed. Children truly were resilient. Amazingly so.

Dillon shifted next to her. His hand closed over her gloveless fingers, warm, strong. "It seems so long since the last time I touched you."

She didn't even try to suppress her laugh. He had touched her while rowing Mylinski's old fishing boat across the narrow backwater channel to the sandbar they now explored. While Amanda had been busy watching out for chunks of ice at the stern, he had kissed his fingertips and pressed them to Jacqueline's lips. She squeezed his hand, reveling in the warmth, the texture of his skin, and tossed him a teasing smile. "I hate to break it to you, cowboy, but it's only been ten minutes since you last touched me."

He returned her smile in kind. "Like I said, too long. Much too long."

A giddiness bubbled up inside her, an effervescence she'd never quite felt before.

Flavors of last night swirled in her mind like complex wine. Her skin still burned this morning from the roughness of his beard stubble. Her thighs still ached from their lovemaking. It had been wonderful. Each moment delicious. And she wanted more. She wanted it to last forever.

She shook thoughts of the future from her mind. There would be plenty of time to deal with reality. To deal with being alone again. To look back. To remember.

Right now she had memories to make.

She tilted her head and shot him a wicked smile. "Wait until I get hold of you tonight. You'll get more touching than you can handle."

He raised his eyebrows. "Is that a promise?"

"No, it's a threat."

His laugh boomed across the flat sandbar. "Now, that's the kind of threat I can live with."

"You won't be laughing tonight."

"Laughing? No, I guarantee I won't be laughing." His eyes smoldered with ideas of what he might be doing instead. He raised her hand to his lips and kissed her palm.

A tingle shot up her arm and over her skin. A delicious promise of what was to come. "I can't wait. But now we'd better catch up with Amanda. She's probably had about enough exploring on her own by now."

"Mommy?" As if on cue, Amanda's little voice

drifted across the sand. She stood near the clump of scrub brush. The chunk of bark still in her hand, she bounced up and down in an impatient jig.

"I'll be right there, punkin." Jacqueline cocked her head in the direction of her daughter. "What did I tell you?"

Dillon nodded and withdrew his hand from hers. "I never doubted you."

Her hand felt cool at the absence of his touch. She fought the urge to throw herself into his arms. Tonight. She would snuggle in his strong arms tonight. She inhaled deeply, drawing the fresh, clean air into her lungs. Now she'd enjoy every giggle from Amanda's lips, every secret smile from Dillon's twinkling eyes. And she would dream about touching Dillon in the dark.

"Mommy!"

Jacqueline's head snapped up. There was an urgency in her daughter's voice. An edge of panic. Fear shot through her. She launched into a sprint.

Dillon ran beside her. It didn't take them long to reach the tangle of scrub brush. Amanda's face was pale, her eyes round with terror. She clutched the hunk of bark like a shield, her little fingernails digging into the rough surface. "There's a man at the cabin. I saw him."

"Drop to the sand. Now," Dillon commanded.

Jacqueline and Amanda did as he said, lying on their bellies in the cold, wet sand and snow. Jacqueline looped her arm over Amanda's back to shield her from danger with her body. The sand's chill pressed against her cheek and seeped through her parka. The chill of dread seeped into her being.

Dillon crouched low next to them. He reached into his pocket and withdrew the revolver. He crept toward the edge of the clump of brush.

"Be careful." Jacqueline's whisper wobbled with fear.

He gave her a reassuring smile. "Damn straight." Hunching low behind the naked branches, he circled the clump of brush and disappeared from sight.

Jacqueline's heart hammered in her chest. She tried to slow her breathing, but her lungs screamed for air. Under her arm, Amanda's shoulders trembled. "It's okay, baby. Dillon is going to find out who the man is. He'll protect us."

Her little girl nodded, almost imperceptibly. "He'll shoot the man, won't he, Mommy? Dillon will shoot the man and kill him?"

"Yes, sweetheart. If he's a bad man, Dillon will shoot him. We'll be safe." She silently prayed that she'd be proven right.

Seconds ticked by. Minutes.

Finally Dillon circled back around the brush, walking fully upright. He swung his arms by his sides, the gun tucked safely out of sight. "It's Mylinski. Everything's okay."

Relief whooshed from Jacqueline's lips on a stream of air. She sat up and helped her little girl up from the sand.

Dillon smiled, a smile she could tell he'd meant to be comforting, reassuring. But the smile wasn't the carefree, devil-may-care smile of a few minutes ago. His eyes were once again filled with worry.

Foreboding replaced her rush of relief. No matter

what Dillon said, the anxiety in his eyes told the true story. Everything wasn't okay.

It was time to face reality.

DILLON STRAINED BACK against the oars, putting all his frustration into the stroke. The boat shot forward, cutting across the current, bringing them closer to the nightmare that waited on the other side. Damn. He didn't want to set foot on the shore. He didn't want the magic he had experienced the past day with Jacqueline and her daughter to end.

But it had to end. He knew that as well as he knew his own damn name. He'd seen the expression on Mylinski's face. Even across the narrow channel of the river he'd recognized bad news.

Jacqueline had recognized it, too. Tension lined her lush mouth. Worry glazed her wide eyes. Amanda cuddled against her mother's side, very still, so different from the chatty, imaginative girl who'd played on the sandbar.

The boat hit the shore with a thud. Mylinski grabbed the rope at the bow, preventing the current from sweeping them downstream. His balding head glistened in the afternoon sun like a full moon on the rise. After shooting Dillon a care-laden look, he plastered a big smile on his face for Amanda. "So, Mandy, did you have fun rowing around the river in old Lizzy here?"

Amanda's eyebrows rose. "Lizzy?"

"Leaking Lizzy." He gestured to the rowboat. "The old girl likes communing with the river bottom."

Amanda looked around the bottom of the boat as if expecting to see the water rising around her ankles.

Mylinski laughed. "Don't worry, Mandy-girl. I just had her all caulked and fixed up for spring."

She still looked anxious to get out of the boat.

Mylinski's methods might leave something to be desired, but Dillon had to give him credit for taking the little girl's mind off her real fear. As well as the somber mood of her mother and himself. He stepped out of the boat and secured it so Jacqueline and Amanda could climb out. He didn't want to look at Jacqueline. He knew what he'd see in her eyes. The same pain she would see in his.

Striding back in the direction of the cabin, Mylinski dipped his hand into the pocket of his overcoat and pulled out a handful of colorful candy. "Look what I just found in my pocket. Would you like some, Mandy?"

Amanda glanced up at Jacqueline.

Jacqueline nodded. "Go ahead, punkin. You may have a piece."

She chose a piece from Mylinski's open hand. "Thank you."

The detective dipped a hand into his other coat pocket. "Would you look at this? I found something in this pocket, too." He pulled out a Barbie doll dressed from head to toe in English riding togs. Amanda's eyes nearly popped out of her head. She held the doll in her little hands, staring at her prize. "Thank you, Dedective," she whispered.

They climbed the steps and entered the cabin. Once Amanda was occupied in the bedroom with her candy, her doll and her stuffed horse, Dillon zeroed in on Mylinski. "Where the hell have you been?"

"New York City. I had to go pick up a guy that skipped bail." Disgust filled Mylinski's voice. "Kearney was supposed to do it, but the little soldier called in sick. Flu or something."

Kearney again. Dillon frowned. "How about the investigation? What have you turned up?"

"Nothing. *Nada.* But that's not the important thing. You guys have got to get out of here."

A shot of adrenaline spiked his bloodstream at the urgency in Mylinski's voice. "What's happened?"

"The department traced the call you made last night from The Riverbend Tavern. They know you're here and they know you have Jacqueline and Amanda. The state police are combing the area as we speak."

Damn. He'd thought he'd been safe making that call from the tavern. Instead he'd led the police right to them. And if the mole in the task force had gotten wind of the trace, Buck Swain was closing in on them, too.

Beside him, eyes rounding with fear as the full meaning of Mylinski's words sank in, Jacqueline glanced in the direction of the bedroom where her little girl played with her new doll. Biting her bottom lip, she searched Dillon's face for reassurance, for comfort, for a plan. "What do we do?"

His gut clenched. He didn't know, but he'd better come up with something. And damned quick. "The first thing we have to do is get Amanda out of the police's reach. Then we'll worry about Swain."

Jacqueline nodded, latching on to his words like a

lifeline. "How do we do that? If the police are sweeping the area, we can't just hop in the car and breeze past them."

Mylinski cleared his throat. "They have the make, model and license plate number of your rental car."

"So what do we do?" Her question hung in the air.

Dillon squeezed her hand in his. "We split up. We send Amanda with Al. He can take her out of state and hide her."

"Send Amanda—" Jacqueline's back stiffened. "I'm not letting Amanda out of my sight."

Mylinski stepped toward her. "Listen to Dillon. His plan is sound."

Dillon grasped both of her hands. "The warrant is issued for you, Jacqueline. Not Amanda. If you two aren't together, the police can't take her in. Al can keep her safe."

Her eyes grew hard as if shutters had slammed closed, not letting his words inside. She shook her head.

Dillon clutched her upper arms. "The police are here, Jacqueline. And Swain's right on their heels. Sending Amanda with Al is my only plan. If you have another one, spit it out."

She gasped air like a drowning woman. Breath after breath.

He raised his hand to her jaw and tilted her face up to his. He looked deep into her troubled eyes. "I trust Al, Jacqueline. You can trust him, too."

Understanding registered in her eyes. As if from sheer will, she drew herself up, swung her gaze to

Mylinski and nodded her head. "Take good care of my baby, Detective."

Mylinski's hazel eyes met hers. He nodded solemnly. "Like she was my own flesh and blood."

Chapter Fifteen

The sun's rays beat hot on Jacqueline's face and glared off the brown water that swirled around the boat and swept them downstream. Silence hung over the river like a pall, broken only by the scrape and thump of the oars as Dillon dipped them into the water and strained back against them. He'd long since shrugged out of his duster. The coat now lay in a heap on the bench at the nose of the boat, its tattered shoulder drooping over the edge. Sweat glistened in the open collar of his white dress shirt.

She pulled her gaze from him and stared blankly at the stuffed horse in her hands. Amanda had insisted she take Dorsey the Horsey with her. She'd promised Dorsey would help keep her safe. Tears pooled in her eyes as she replayed the memory of Amanda's brave little face looking back from the window of Mylinski's sedan as he drove down the rutted dirt road. Her arms ached for the feel of her little girl.

And her heart ached for what she and Dillon had lost.

Pain settled deep into Jacqueline's bones. It was

over. All over. The peace. The happiness. The joy she'd found with Dillon and Amanda in that cabin along the river. All gone. Shattered into jagged pieces that slashed into her heart.

"Amanda will be all right," Dillon said, breaking the painful silence, his voice thick with sympathy. "Al will take good care of her."

She looked up. Dillon, the river and the boat were nothing but a watery blur of color through the haze of unshed tears. She blinked, trying to clear her vision. "I know."

"But knowing doesn't make letting her go any easier."

"No, it doesn't." She glanced away from him and brushed her eyes with the back of her hand. "None of it is easy. Letting her go. Or letting you go."

Dillon grimaced. He paused, and for a moment she thought he might drop the oars and take her in his arms once more.

Her heart strained in her chest. What she wouldn't give to lay her head against his chest and listen to the vital beat of his heart. To draw in his scent. To taste the magic of his kiss.

But she couldn't. Not now. Not anymore. She hugged the stuffed horse close. "I'm sorry."

"I'm sorry, too." He tore his eyes from hers and turned to glance downriver.

Jacqueline followed his gaze, glad to have something to focus on, something to take her mind off the ache that burrowed into her heart and echoed in her soul. The stark lines of a railroad bridge loomed ahead, etched against the brown of the river and the blue of the sky.

Dillon turned back to face her and gave the oars a strong pull. "Spring Green is just ahead. We can call for a rental car there and drive to the Iowa border. Amanda and Mylinski will be waiting in Mount Hosmer Park near Lansing, Iowa. Before you know it, you'll have Amanda back in your arms."

"And then what? A state line may take care of the police, but it won't stop Swain."

"Then you and Amanda disappear until I find some way to nail Swain. Can you stay with your mother in Germany?"

"She'd be thrilled."

"Then as soon as we pick up Amanda, we'll get the two of you on a plane."

And she and Dillon would say goodbye.

He plunged the oars into the water and pulled back, propelling the boat with the current. "The sooner we get off this river, the better. I feel like a sitting-damn-duck out here."

Pulling her gaze from him, she focused on the trees inhabiting the banks on either side of the river. The river birches with their shaggy bark. The oaks with their gnarled branches. The river bluffs loomed like blue shadows all around them.

A clammy chill spread over her skin. Just this morning she'd thought the river and its banks beautiful, peaceful. But now everywhere she looked she saw Swain hiding among those naked branches, watching them, lining them up in his sights.

"What if we don't make it? What if the police find us?" Or, worse yet, Swain? She let that thought go unspoken.

Dillon offered her a reassuring smile. "Al is prepared to hide Amanda for as long as it takes for me to straighten out the material-witness-warrant mess. Don't worry. She's going to be okay.''

A shot rang out.

''Get down!'' He surged toward her and pulled her down to the floor of the rowboat. She flattened against the cold metal, Dillon's heavy body on top of her, shielding her. Another shot echoed off the bluffs.

Swain had found them.

DILLON REACHED for the gun tucked securely in the waistband of his jeans. His worst nightmare had come true. Damn. A sandbar upstream had forced them to swing wide, away from the protective branches along the shore. Swain had found them on the river where they had no protection, no cover of any kind.

But he hadn't hit them.

''The bastard's toying with us. Like an old tomcat toys with an injured mouse.''

Beneath him, Jacqueline nodded. ''Maybe he thinks we'll lead him to Amanda.'' Her muffled voice rang with a note of fear.

''Well, he's wrong. And he's not going to get us, either.'' He raised the Defender above the side of the boat, its grip slippery in his sweaty hand.

The sharp crack of the rifle echoed off the bluffs.

The Defender jumped from his grasp and fell into the river. Pain burned like fire in Dillon's hand. Blood trickled over his wrist and soaked into the sleeve of his shirt like red dye.

That shot was true enough.

A fourth shot rang out. A bullet ripped through the side of the boat. Water poured in through the hole, arching like the stream of a drinking fountain.

They had to get off this damned river. They had to find cover. "We're going to have to swim for it."

Jacqueline stared wide-eyed at the hole only inches from her head. Nodding, she shucked her coat.

"Leave your boots on. They're hell to swim in, but we'll need them once we reach shore."

Another shot tore through the boat's aluminum hull.

Water filled the boat, inch after frigid inch, cold as death. The boat listed, one side rising in the air. A little more and it would swamp. Dillon grabbed Jacqueline's hand, squeezing her fingers in his. "We'll tip out and roll into the river. That way the boat will act like a shield between us and Swain."

Jacqueline nodded.

"Ready?"

She stared him straight in the eye. Unflinching. A warrior's look. "Ready."

As one, they rolled out of the boat and into the river.

The water's chill grabbed Dillon like a steel fist. The powerful current pulled at him, sweeping him downstream. He held tight to Jacqueline's hand, her warmth a lifeline in the swirling, frigid water.

Another shot split the air and kicked up a splash of water mere inches from Dillon's head. His heart slammed against his ribs.

Next to them the disabled boat hovered low in the water, sinking fast. Soon there would be nothing to hide behind. Nothing to protect them from Swain's fire.

And the cold. Mind-numbing, life-sapping cold. His body ached from it, his hands and feet going numb. Jacqueline shivered next to him, her lips blue. Soon their bodies would start shutting down to conserve heat. They had to get out of the water soon. Very soon. Or they would be just two more chunks of ice floating to the Mississippi.

If Swain didn't get them first.

The steel beams of the railroad bridge loomed in front of them. "The bridge. We'll climb out there. The girders will prevent Swain from getting a clear shot."

Jacqueline nodded and said something, her teeth chattering so loudly he couldn't make out the words.

The river carried them closer and closer to the bridge. He tensed his muscles, willing them to work despite the cold. As the current swept them under the steel beams, he dropped Jacqueline's hand and grabbed a cement pylon anchoring the structure in the riverbed. The surface was slimy with algae. His fingers slipped, then caught, digging into a jagged edge.

The river bore Jacqueline along behind him. She grabbed for the pylon. Her fingers slipped. The disabled boat rushed by on the current. He reached for her hand. His numbed fingers closed around her wrist and slipped in the cold.

No. He couldn't lose her. He forced his fingers to close tighter, grip harder. He pulled her toward him. The current pulled back, threatening to rip her from his grasp. Finally her fingers touched the pylon, gripped and held on.

For a moment all he could do was cling to the slippery cement, breath coming in clouded puffs. His limbs too tired, too numb to move. His mind hazy as if mired in a dream.

Next to him, Jacqueline's whole body quaked with cold, her skin white, her lips blue. He had to concentrate. He had to think. Somehow, he had to get them out of this damned water.

He reached for the girders above his head, his arms heavy, clumsy with cold. With one hand and then the other, he grasped the frigid steel and lifted his body out of the current.

Throwing a leg over the girder, he reached down for Jacqueline. "Give me your hand."

She bit her lower lip, stilling its uncontrolled tremble. With a grimace she managed to reach high enough for him to grasp her hand.

He pulled her up to the girder. Slowly they inched up the cold steel framework until they crouched exhausted on the tracks, hidden behind a steel beam. Below, the river swirled and gurgled around the feet of the bridge.

Dillon squinted downriver. The town was still a good distance away, a cluster of houses visible at the foot of a bluff. Swain was likely closing in on them this very moment. Their only chance was to get to town as quickly as possible. "We still have a couple of miles to go. Are you up to it?"

Jacqueline nodded, wrapping her arms around herself in a futile effort to conserve body heat. "I'm up to anything. Just get me to Amanda.'' Her words slurred with cold.

They crawled along the tracks, steel colder than ice against their hands and knees. Finally the swell of the bank rose to meet the steel beams. Scraggly sumac closed in on either side of the tracks. No rustle of movement. No sign of Swain. Dillon struggled to his feet and helped Jacqueline stand beside him.

The purr of a car motor rose over the vibrato of the rushing current below. Dillon spun in the direction of the sound.

A white Lexus glided up the rough gravel road toward them.

An uneasy tightness descended on the muscles in Dillon's neck and shoulders. Neil Fitzroy's car. He would recognize it anywhere. What the hell was Fitz doing here?

The car stopped and the door swung wide. Fitz burst out. Eyebrows pinched and lips locked in a snarl, he stalked down the tracks toward them.

Jacqueline grew rigid beside him. ''That's your boss, isn't it? What do we do now?'' Her voice edged high with panic. Her words slurred with cold.

''Let me handle him.''

She nodded and rubbed her hands up and down her arms in a futile attempt to warm herself.

Dillon zeroed in on the district attorney. ''You promised me forty-eight hours, Fitz.''

He came to a halt in front of them, narrowed his eyes on Dillon and stuffed his hands into the pockets of his overcoat. ''Where's the girl, Reese?''

The tension in Dillon's shoulders sharpened. ''She's safe. Like I've been telling you all along, I'll take care of this. You didn't have to issue that damned warrant.''

His eyes darted from Dillon to Jacqueline and back again. He cleared his throat, his voice rough with impatience. ''Obviously I did. Care to explain why you decided to take a swim in the river in the middle of February, for God's sake? You've forced us to divert valuable resources away from apprehending Swain and his informant.''

''Apprehending?'' Dillon latched on to the word. A shot of adrenaline spiked his blood. ''Do you know who the informant is?''

''As a matter of fact, we do. Now we just have to find him.''

Him. That ruled out Kit Ashner. ''Harrington? Has he disappeared?''

Fitz shook his head curtly, his mouth twitching with disappointment. ''Swain's informant isn't Harrington.''

Dillon's mind raced. ''Then who?''

''You mean you haven't figured it out?'' Fitz shook his head as if disappointed in Dillon's deductive powers. ''No, of course you wouldn't have. He would be the last person you'd suspect. The informant is Al Mylinski.''

Chapter Sixteen

A scream rose in Jacqueline's throat. No. It couldn't be true. Al Mylinski couldn't be Swain's informant. He had her baby. *Her baby.* If he was working with Swain—

She looked to Dillon.

He didn't even glance at her, his attention riveted on the district attorney. "Where did you get that damn fool idea?"

"I knew you wouldn't believe me. That's why I put out the warrant. I wanted to get Mrs. Schettler and her daughter in protective custody before the detective returned from his trip to New York. Now, where's the little girl?"

Trembling inside and out, Jacqueline opened her mouth to speak.

Dillon threw up a hand to silence her. "Why do you think Mylinski is the informant? What evidence do you have?"

"After the antics you've pulled the past few days and your personal ties to the detective, do you really expect me to lay the evidence out for you? Where's your head, Reese? If you haven't figured it out by

now, you're officially off this case." He turned to
Jacqueline, his gaze cutting into her, sharp and
pointed as a laser. "Where is your daughter, Mrs.
Schettler?"

Jacqueline's head spun. She should be able to feel
if Amanda was all right, shouldn't she? She should
be able to feel it in her heart. In her soul. But she
felt nothing. Nothing but the cold edge of dread.
Nothing but bloodcurdling fear.

Had she put her baby in the hands of a murderer?

A chill claimed her, more bitter than the icy water
of the river. She looked to Dillon. For answers. For
reassurance. For anything.

Gaze riveted on the district attorney, Dillon didn't
meet her eyes. A muscle along his jaw clenched, but
his eyes betrayed no emotion.

Look at me, damn it, her mind screamed. *Look at
me.* But she couldn't force a sound from her lips.
Panic shot through her, strong as searing pain. Her
knees trembled. Her heart felt as if it would explode.
Look at me.

Neil Fitzroy watched her closely, as if dissecting
her every movement. A deep frown creased his forehead. "You gave your daughter to Detective Mylinski, didn't you, Mrs. Schettler?"

A strangled whimper issued from her throat. She
covered her mouth with her hand. *Look at me, Dillon.*
She reached out and touched his arm.

"Where did Detective Mylinski take her, Mrs.
Schettler? There might still be time to stop him."

Dillon finally turned to look at her. His eyes were
calm, deep and dark.

And then she knew.

She didn't have faith in the police. She didn't have faith in the district attorney. She didn't have faith in the system.

But she had faith in Dillon.

And if despite what Neil Fitzroy said Dillon still trusted Al Mylinski, then so did she.

She drew in a shaky breath, raised her chin and met Fitzroy's eyes. "I don't know where he took her. I can't tell you anything."

DILLON TOOK IN THE TILT to Jacqueline's chin, the confidence in her eyes. She trusted him. Even with her daughter's life on the line, she trusted him.

And he couldn't let her down.

Turning back to Fitz, Dillon narrowed his eyes on the district attorney. Pressure pierced the back of his neck like a rattler sinking in its fangs. "Why are you so hell-bent on tracking down Mylinski? If he is working with Swain as you say, there isn't a chance in hell that Amanda's still alive."

"Maybe not, but do you want to take that chance, Reese?" He turned his eyes on Jacqueline. "Do you, Mrs. Schettler?"

Unflinching, she returned his scrutiny.

Anger tinged Fitz's hairline red. A snarl contorted his movie-star face. "What is wrong with you people? I know Mylinski is your friend, Reese, but you can't sacrifice a little girl's life out of some kind of misplaced loyalty. Where did he take her?" His voice cracked with rage. With desperation.

Desperation.

Events flashed through Dillon's mind. Jancy's aborted interview with Mark Schettler. Val's not-so-secret location. Mylinski's sudden orders to fly to New York. The material-witness warrant for Jacqueline. Fitz had a controlling hand in every situation.

And Swain's well-placed shots on the river. He hadn't been merely toying with them. He'd been driving them like cattle. To the railroad bridge. To Fitz.

Son of a bitch, *Fitz* was the informant.

Dillon looked into Fitz's red-rimmed eyes. Revulsion clenched his gut. Why hadn't he seen it before? "Does Swain have us lined up in his sights right now, Fitz?"

Fitz didn't move. There was no sound except Jacqueline's sharp intake of breath.

"Did you order him to pull the trigger as soon as I tell you where Amanda is? Or will he wait until we lead you to her? What's the plan, Fitz? Surely you've worked this out."

Fitz stared at him as if he really didn't have a clue what Dillon was talking about. His eyes darted from Dillon to Jacqueline and back again. "Is this some kind of joke?"

Dillon didn't buy the innocent act for a moment. "I have a better sense of humor than that. The only thing I can't figure out is why in Sam Hill did you get into league with Swain in the first place? You're the district attorney—why would you feed information to some two-bit criminal?"

Fitz sank his hands into the pockets of his overcoat. "I don't know what you're talking about, Reese. Now, are we just going to sit around and talk nonsense, or are we going to rescue the Schettler girl?"

"Rescue?" Dillon almost choked on the word. "I doubt rescue is what you have in mind."

A lighter struck flint, and cigarette smoke wafted toward them like a bad omen. "It sure as hell isn't what I have in mind." The smoke-roughened voice came from behind them, out of the tangle of sumac at the edge of the railroad tracks.

Jacqueline gasped.

Dillon's gut clenched. Slowly he turned around. "Hello, Swain."

Dressed head to toe in camouflage fatigues that were soaked to the waist, Buck Swain strode out of the tangle of naked trees and brush. He cradled a military-style sniper's rifle in his arms, the barrel pointed directly at Jacqueline's chest. His finger was poised over the trigger, the skin of his hand and arm scarred red and slick from the wartime heroics that had earned him the Purple Heart. "Hello, Reese. Long time no see. You look a little pale."

Dillon stared into Swain's eyes, dead and black as a devil's straight out of hell.

"What? Nothing to say?" Swain clenched the cigarette between thin lips. Smoke rose from the tip and curled around his head. "Not as talkative as you were in court, eh, Reese? But then, you don't have a jury to lie to here."

Jacqueline shifted closer to Dillon. Eyes narrowed into slits, she glared at Swain. Her clenched fists trembled at her sides.

Dillon turned to locate Fitz. The D.A. faced him from the crook of his vehicle's open door, a .38 nestled comfortably in his hand. Dillon had figured out the identity of Swain's informant, but he'd done it too late. Too late for him. Too late for justice.

And too late for the woman he loved.

He looked to Jacqueline. Shivering from cold and fear, she stared Swain straight in the eye and raised her chin a notch.

Dillon swallowed into a dry throat. He loved her. With every fiber of his body, his heart, his soul. And it couldn't be too late for her, for them. He wouldn't *let* it be too late.

He swung his gaze to Fitz. Anger surged up inside him. Blistering anger. "How could you do it, Fitz? How could you help a snake like him?"

Swain raised an eyebrow in Fitz's direction. "You mean he didn't tell you? We're business partners from way back. Fitzroy here is one corrupt son of a bitch. I brought him the poor, downtrodden criminals, and he fixed their cases. For a price."

Fixing cases. Selling justice. Bile rose in Dillon's throat. Under all that polished political veneer the man was as rotten as any murderer he'd ever put behind bars. "Why, Fitz?"

"In a word?" Fitz said, his voice measured, precise, as if he was explaining the rules of evidence to a first-year law student. "Money. Money to look like a winner. To live in Maple Bluff, to drive the right car, to buy the right boat, to afford the friends that can put me in the district attorney's office. The state senate. Or the governor's mansion."

Political ambition. It had always been Fitz's weakness. Dillon just hadn't realized how deep and how twisted Fitz's ambition had become. "And Harrington? Was he responsible for letting Swain's foster brother off with a slap on the wrist, or was that you, too?''

Fitz crooked a sardonic brow. "Harrington was fresh out of law school and more idealistic than he should have been. He was easy to manipulate.''

"And the leak in that armed robbery case? Was that you, too?''

Fitz shrugged, as if he'd been caught doing nothing more heinous than jaywalking.

Abhorrence washed through Dillon in a wave. Just the sight of Fitz turned his stomach. "And to think I believed you cared about justice.''

"Face it, Dillon. There's no such thing as justice. Not for victims, not for their families, not even for the criminals. The system is about making deals. Pure and simple. But I never meant for it to lead to this.''

Swain let out a bitter bark of a laugh. "To murder? No. You never had the guts for anything like murder. It was up to me to keep things under wraps. To do what needed to be done.''

Fitzroy focused a condescending sneer on Swain. "And if you had done a better job in the first place, it wouldn't have had to go so far.''

For a moment Swain looked as though he might turn his weapon on Fitzroy and put a bullet in his accomplice right then and there. Instead, he knocked the ash off his cigarette and took a long drag. "The only blood on my hands is Liz's. My darling Liz who stumbled on our little enterprise. And I wouldn't have offed her if she hadn't been going to talk to the attorney general.''

Liz Kroll. Swain's first victim. The one who had

started the dominoes falling. Dillon could still picture her bloody body, still see the ribbon of red across her throat, the precise stab wound in her heart. The scene had been stripped of evidence. No murder weapon, no fingerprints, no fibers of any use. If Mark Schettler hadn't seen Swain tossing his bloody clothing into the Dumpster behind the Schettler Brew Pub, Swain would have gotten away free as the snake who killed Janey.

Beside Dillon, Jacqueline shifted, her boot soles grinding against gravel. "You admit you killed that woman?"

"Yeah. I did Liz. But your husband? Reese got him killed. Reese and his trial. And that bartender, too. Just like Reese and his trial are forcing me to kill you and your little girl."

Jacqueline bristled, and for a moment Dillon thought she might launch herself at Swain, rifle or no. But she remained rooted to the spot, eyes shooting daggers. "Leave Amanda alone. She won't be any danger to you."

"I gave you a chance to run. A chance to keep your kid safe. But you didn't take it. It ain't only Reese's fault. Your daughter's blood will be on your hands, too."

Jacqueline took a step toward Swain before Dillon could grab her.

Swain chuckled and raised the gun barrel, aiming at Jacqueline's face. "I'd stop if I were you, Jackie. Unless you want to make your daughter an orphan right now."

She stopped, her body rigid. "You bastard."

"I've been called worse. Just ask your boyfriend here. He's called me worse in open court."

Dillon willed Jacqueline to remain still, keep silent. He wanted to pull her behind him, shield her from Swain with his body. But he didn't dare move, didn't dare breathe, didn't dare do anything that could set Swain off and give him an excuse to pull the trigger.

"Quit screwing around, Swain," Fitz said, his voice tight, riding the edge. "You're wasting time. Get serious. We need to find out where the girl is. Al Mylinski is hiding her."

Swain brushed Fitz's voice away with a twitch of his head, as if he was brushing away the annoying buzz of a fly. He kept the rifle barrel steady, pointed straight between Jacqueline's eyes. "I waited far too long for this moment. Didn't I, Reese? I listened to far too many of your lies, your insults. I'm a hero, damn it. A war hero. And you made me look like Satan himself. You're not going to get off easy on this."

Fitz's sigh of disgust echoed through the still air. "No, of course not. You want to wait until some hapless witness stumbles across us so you have to kill him, too. You bungling idiot."

Swain's face grew red. He swung the rifle to face Fitz. A pop split Dillon's eardrums and echoed off the river bluffs.

Fitz slumped against the Lexus and slid to the ground.

Jacqueline gasped and shuddered, staring at Fitz's crumpled body.

Unthinkingly, Dillon reached for her. His hand

closed around her wrist. He had to get her away from Swain, away from—

The rifle barrel swung around, focusing once again on Jacqueline. "Trying to protect your lady, eh, Reese? Touching, but not so fast. Let go of her. I'm not done with the two of you."

Dillon dropped Jacqueline's wrist.

"Over there, Jackie." Swain motioned to the white Lexus with a nod of his head. "Just in case your boyfriend has any heroics in mind."

Jacqueline moved away from Dillon, to the spot Swain had indicated. Eyes on Swain, she stumbled on Fitzroy's body and fell to the ground beside him.

"Get up," Swain ordered. "Unless you want a bullet in your back."

She scrambled to her feet. She raised her chin and looked at Dillon. Large and round with fear, her eyes still held a spark of fire.

His lady had guts.

She glanced down and then back to Dillon. He followed her gaze. Fitz was turned slightly to the side, the butt of his .38 poking from under his still body.

Determination solidified inside Dillon, hard as iron. He had to find some way to reach the gun. Some way to save Jacqueline. Some way to save them both. "Now you've done it, Swain."

"Done what? Killed him?" Swain nodded to Fitz's still body. "Never mind him. He would have made a lousy governor, anyway."

"That's not what I'm talking about." Dillon forced a cocky smile to his lips. "With Fitz you had a direct pipeline into the D.A.'s office, you had a chance of finding the little girl. Now that he's dead, you're out of luck. If you want to find her, I guess you'll have to keep us alive."

Instead of slipping, Swain's smirk just grew wider. "Reese, Reese, Reese. You're familiar with modern surveillance equipment, aren't you? There are nice little devices that let a person listen in on a conversation, even when the people talking are in the middle of a river." He turned his eyes to the bright blue sky. "It's an awful nice day to play in Mount Hosmer Park, isn't it?"

Dillon's insides went cold. Mylinski and Amanda were sitting ducks for Swain and his rifle. It was over. All over.

Unless he could get his hands on Fitz's gun. But to do so, he'd have to reach Fitz's body. Impossible with the barrel of Swain's rifle pointed square at Jacqueline, his finger poised on the trigger. Swain would shoot her before Dillon could take his second step.

But Dillon would have to find a way. "What do you want, Swain?"

"I want to enjoy the victory. I want you to admit I've won." A full-fledged grin crept over his face, showing an even row of nicotine-yellowed teeth. He threw back his head and belted out a harsh laugh. "Can you feel it? I sure can. It feels sweet. It feels like justice."

Justice. The word left Dillon cold. What the hell did Swain know about justice? Or Fitz, either? Their ideas of justice were as distorted and crooked as snakes in a cactus patch.

He glanced at Jacqueline. Her blue lips, her teeth

chattering with cold, her narrowed eyes burning with rage and strength and love.

Was his own idea of justice any better? Or was it just as warped?

Ten years. Hundreds of cases. Punishing Janey's killer with each one. Punishing himself.

His need for vengeance had so blinded him he hadn't even realized he loved Jacqueline until it was too late. Too late to take her in his arms. Too late to tell her how he felt. Too late to make this twisted nightmare turn out differently.

He wanted Jacqueline and Amanda safe in his arms, for now and for always. He wanted a new chance at life. For them and for him. A chance to make up for the mistakes of the past. A chance to forge a new future. A future of love. Love Amanda deserved. Love Jacqueline deserved.

Love *he* deserved.

And he sure as hell wasn't going to let Swain rob him of that chance.

Swain leveled the barrel of his weapon on Dillon. "Say it, Reese. I've won. I've beat you. I want to hear it from your lips."

Dillon set his feet, tensed his muscles to launch himself at Swain. "Go to hell."

A shot rang out.

Too late. Dillon steeled himself for the hot pain of a bullet slicing through his flesh.

But the pain never came.

Instead, Jacqueline plowed into Swain, sending his shot wild.

This was his chance.

Dillon leapt for Fitz's body. His fingers closed

over the .38. He swung around, pointing the gun just as Swain focused the barrel of his rifle on Jacqueline.

Dillon squeezed the trigger. The .38 jumped in his hand. Once. Twice.

And Swain slumped to the ground.

Chapter Seventeen

"Jacqueline." Dillon closed his hand over her trembling shoulder. "It's over, darlin'. Swain's dead."

She stared straight ahead, her eyes seeing but not seeing. Finally she tore her gaze from Swain's crumpled form. She looked up at Dillon, her wide, haunted eyes searching his. Her face was pale, her skin as white and delicate as tissue paper. "He was going to kill you."

Dillon gathered her in his arms and held her shivering body close. "Thanks to you, I'm all right."

Cheek pressed against his chest, she bit her bottom lip. "You shot him."

"Yes."

She shook her head as if this was an unacceptable answer, an unthinkable answer. "I'm glad. A man is dead. I should feel sorry. I should feel guilty. But all I feel is relieved."

"He would have killed us. He would have killed Amanda. You *should* feel relieved. I feel relieved, too."

Drawing back from his arms, she tilted her head back and looked into his eyes. Some of the color had already returned to her cheeks. She nodded and blew a stream of air through pursed lips. "We're safe now. Amanda's finally safe."

"Yes." He lowered his head and brushed her cold lips with his. A kiss of gratitude. A kiss of promise. Promise for the future. "I have to call the police. Will you be all right here for a moment?"

She drew herself up and set that strong jaw of hers. "I'm fine. I'll be fine."

"I'll just be a moment." He moved to the white Lexus and opened the door. Using Fitz's cell phone, he called 911. A quick rummage through the back seat produced a blanket and a pair of warm boots, required equipment for winter driving in Wisconsin. He gathered the blanket and boots and returned to Jacqueline's side.

Once he'd replaced her soaked boots with the large insulated ones and wrapped the blanket around her shoulders, he ushered her away from the blood. Away from the death.

He'd gotten everything he could have hoped for. Jacqueline's life. Amanda's life. His life. And a second chance at a future. And now it was up to him to make that chance count.

He motioned to a fallen tree on the edge of the forest. They sank onto the log. Jacqueline wrapped part of the blanket around him, and they huddled together under its warmth.

He took her hands in his. He had to make this good. He had to make her understand what was in his heart. Because his new shot at life, at a future, didn't exist without her. "I've been a damned idiot."

A little crease appeared between her eyebrows and

she looked at him as if he was speaking another language.

"I've given up everything for justice. I've turned a blind eye to everything. And not just my own happiness. I've ignored how my obsession affects other people. Innocent people. Janey believed in helping people. She believed in family. She believed in love. In my crusade to avenge her death, I've gone against everything Janey believed in. Everything *I* believed in."

Jacqueline raised a hand to his face and smoothed her fingers along his jaw. Her touch reached into him and moved his heart.

"You asked me once if Janey would want me to be happy and have a family, and she would. More than anything. It would be the best gift I could give her. And the best gift I could give myself."

He swallowed into a dry throat. He had to make her believe. "When Swain had his gun on you, when I thought I was going to lose you—" His voice cracked with emotion. "I want to start living again, Jacqueline. I want to be happy. I want a family. I want you."

She drew in a sharp breath. Tears hovered in her eyes. She opened her mouth to speak.

He pressed a finger to her lips. "Don't say anything. Let me finish." He moved his finger from her mouth, trailing a caress over her strong jaw and down the silken column of her neck. "A lot has changed in the last twenty-four hours. I've changed. I can see things clearly now. More clearly than I've ever been able to in my life. And right now I'm looking at the woman I want to spend the rest of my life with."

She drew in a sharp breath and tilted her face up to his.

He looked into eyes bluer than God's blue sky and deeper than his ocean. "I love you, Jacqueline. And I want us to be together—you, Amanda and me. I want us to be a family."

A smile spread over her lips and dented one smooth cheek. "Are you finished?"

An answering smile blossomed on his face. "Yes, I'm finished."

"Good. Because if I have to wait one more minute to tell you I love you, I'll burst."

A bolt of happiness shook him to the soles of his boots. He pulled her into his arms and kissed her the way she should be kissed. With his whole heart. With his whole soul. When he finally ended the kiss, it was only because he had a question he was burning to ask. A question he needed her to answer. "And will you marry me?"

She pursed her lips in a thoughtful pose. "That depends."

"Depends on what?"

"On what a certain little girl has to say about a new daddy. But from all indications, she's as crazy about you as her mom is."

"So that's a definite maybe, huh?"

She gave him a decisive nod. "A definite maybe."

"You know I won't stop until I get my way."

She tossed him an amused smile. A beautiful smile full of hope and love and promise for the future. "Yeah, I noticed that about you."

He was grinning like a jackass eating thistle, but he couldn't seem to help himself. He took her in his arms and drew her close. He couldn't get enough of her, the feel of her softness in his arms, the scent of her vanilla fragrance, the sound of her soft breathing. His heart danced in his chest, and joy lifted his soul.

He'd finally set things right.

Epilogue

Jacqueline looked around the small crowd gathered in the main dining room of the Schettler Brew Pub. People chatted, glasses of honey Maibock and champagne dangling from their fingers. White roses and lilies topped nearby tables and cascaded from the corners of the oak bar. The lace and chiffon of her wedding dress rustled deliciously with her every movement. Everything was perfect. Just perfect.

Except that just when she needed Dillon, he was nowhere to be seen.

"Mom?"

Amanda peered up at her under the tattered remnants of what used to be a beautiful wreath of freesia in her hair, her cheeks pink with excitement.

"Hi, punkin. What have you been up to?"

"Playing. Dillon gave me some quarters for the pinball machine downstairs."

Jacqueline almost shook her head. Dillon was a painfully easy mark for Amanda. He couldn't say no to her daughter if his life depended on it. Of course, his fun-loving indulgences had helped replace Amanda's bad memories of the brew pub with new happy ones, and she couldn't argue with that. Her little girl was back and blossoming like never before. "Where is Dillon now, sweetheart?"

She shrugged. "I dunno. Listen, Mom, Dedective Mylinski wants to give me some candy."

Jacqueline frowned. That darned "dedective" and his sweet tooth. "Does he, now?"

"Yes. But he wanted me to ask you first. Can I have some?"

"May I," she corrected, trying to look stern.

"May I?"

"One piece. We're going to have cake soon, too, punkin."

"Cake? All right!" Amanda exclaimed as she scampered away.

Jacqueline couldn't help but smile. By the time her daughter finished her candy and cake, she'd be bouncing off the walls with sugar energy. Jacqueline would probably have to tie her down.

Oh well, let her have her fun. After all, it wasn't every day a little girl got a brand-new daddy. And her mommy married the man she loved. Jacqueline felt like bouncing off the walls herself.

Instead she let the smile spread over her face until she was beaming like the sun on a cloudless day, and scanned the room again for Dillon.

It wasn't like him to disappear when she needed him. He'd been there for her every day since Mark's death. He'd helped her move on. The past two months had been hard, but she'd gotten through them. Dillon, Amanda and she had gotten through them. Together. She pushed thoughts of the past from her mind. She wouldn't dwell on those memories any longer. She had a wonderful new life to live.

And a husband to locate.

She moved through the crowd, dodging Kit Ashner's animated conversation with Dale Kearney and Dex Harrington and the statuesque Britt Alcott's private tête-à-tête with her husband, Jack—all people Jacqueline had grown to know and like over the past months.

Jacqueline couldn't help noticing the slight bulge of Britt's tummy under her simple yet elegant ice-blue sheath. She remembered Britt's gentle enthusiasm when dealing with Amanda. She would make a wonderful mother. And judging by the way Jack fussed over his wife, he would be a loving father, as well.

She moved past the crowd and to the window overlooking the beer garden. Below, bridal wreath bushes drooped under the weight of their frothy white flowers and cheery yellow daffodils turned their colorful faces to the sky. The stirring excitement of spring permeated the air.

Finally the long winter had ended and spring had come. And finally she was married to the man she loved. She twirled the wedding ring on her finger and smiled.

A door opened below and Dillon stepped out onto the cobblestones, his hands stuffed in the pockets of his tuxedo. At the sight of him, Jacqueline's heart swelled to near bursting. She turned from the window and scampered down the stairs to the garden below.

Once outside, she walked up behind him and

curved her arms around his waist, hugging his warmth to her. "I need you, cowboy."

He folded his arms over hers. "I need you, too. To make me happy for the rest of my life."

"I need you for more than that."

He turned around to face her and read the serious look on her face. His dark brows slashed over his eyes. "Anything you need, I'll give it to you. You know that."

"Good. Then you can't refuse. This is very hard for me to say, but—" She couldn't stifle the teasing smile that spread over her lips. "I need you to come inside and cut our wedding cake."

He smiled. "I don't know. That may be a little much to ask."

She slapped him playfully in the arm with an open palm.

He grabbed her and encircled her in his arms. "I wish Janey could have met you. And Amanda. She would have loved the two of you. Almost as much as I do."

"And we would have loved her."

"Yes."

She laid her cheek against the lapel of his tux. Safe. Secure. She had everything she wanted. Everything she needed. A smile spread over her lips. Warmth radiated through her soul.

And for that—the smile, the warmth, the love—she had her cowboy to thank.

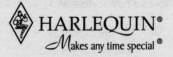

Where the bond of family, tradition and honor run as deep and are as vast as the great Lone Star state, that's...

Texas families are at the heart of the next Harlequin 12-book continuity series.

HARLEQUIN®
INTRIGUE

is proud to launch this brand-new series of books by some of your very favorite authors.

Look for

SOMEONE S BABY
by Dani Sinclair
On sale May 2001

SECRET BODYGUARD
by B.J. Daniels
On sale June 2001

UNCONDITIONAL SURRENDER
by Joanna Wayne
On sale July 2001

Available at your favorite retail outlet.

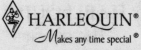

HARLEQUIN®
Makes any time special ®

Visit us at www.eHarlequin.com

HITT

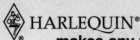

In August 2001

New York Times bestselling author

TESS GERRITSEN

joins

ANNETTE BROADRICK

&

Mary Lynn Baxter

in

TAKE5

Volume 4

These five riveting love stories are quick reads, great escapes and guarantee five times the suspense.

Plus

With $5.00 worth of coupons inside, this is one *exciting* deal!

HARLEQUIN®

Makes any time special ®

Visit us at www.eHarlequin.com

HNCPV4R

Harlequin invites you to walk down the aisle...

To honor our year long celebration of weddings, we are offering an exciting opportunity for you to own the Harlequin Bride Doll. Handcrafted in fine bisque porcelain, the wedding doll is dressed for her wedding day in a cream satin gown accented by lace trim. She carries an exquisite traditional bridal bouquet and wears a cathedral-length dotted Swiss veil. Embroidered flowers cascade down her lace overskirt to the scalloped hemline; underneath all is a multi-layered crinoline.

Join us in our celebration of weddings by sending away for your own Harlequin Bride Doll. This doll regularly retails for $74.95 U.S./approx. $108.68 CDN. One doll per household. Requests must be received no later than December 31, 2001. Offer good while quantities of gifts last. Please allow 6-8 weeks for delivery. Offer good in the U.S. and Canada only. Become part of this exciting offer!

**Simply complete the order form and mail to:
"A Walk Down the Aisle"**

IN U.S.A
P.O. Box 9057
3010 Walden Ave.
Buffalo, NY 14269-9057

IN CANADA
P.O. Box 622
Fort Erie, Ontario
L2A 5X3

Enclosed are eight (8) proofs of purchase found in the last pages of every specially marked Harlequin series book and $3.75 check or money order (for postage and handling). Please send my Harlequin Bride Doll to:

Name (PLEASE PRINT)

Address   Apt. #

City   State/Prov.   Zip/Postal Code

Account # (if applicable)   **097 KIK DAEW**

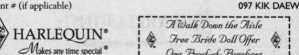

HARLEQUIN®
Makes any time special®

*A Walk Down the Aisle
Free Bride Doll Offer
One Proof-of-Purchase*

Visit us at www.eHarlequin.com   PHWDAPOPR2